ABOUT THE AUTHOR

When Chris Behrsin isn't out exploring the world, he's behind a keyboard writing tales of dragons and magical lands. Born into the genre through a steady diet of Terry Pratchett, his fiction fuses a love for fantasy and whimsical plots with philosophy and voyages into the worlds of dreams.

You can learn more about his fiction and download two free books at his website, chrisbehrsin.com.

facebook.com/chrisbehrsin

x.com/chrisbehrsin

goodreads.com/cbehrsin

bookbub.com/authors/chris-behrsin

BOOKS BY CHRIS BEHRSIN

DRAGONCAT SERIES

A Cat's Guide to Bonding with Dragons

A Cat's Guide to Meddling with Magic

A Cat's Guide to Saving the Kingdom

A Cat's Guide to Questing for Treasure

A Cat's Guide to Travelling through Portals

A Cat's Guide to Vanquishing Evil

A Cat's Guide to Dreaming of Fairies

A Cat's Guide to Dealing with Destiny

A Cat's Guide to Serving a Warlock (Prequel Novella)

SECICAO BLIGHT SERIES

Sukina's Story (Prequel Novel)

Dragonseer

Dragonseers and Bloodlines

Dragonseers and Automatons

Dragonseers and Evolution

More works available at: https://chrisbehrsin.com

DRAGONCAT BOOK 6

A CAT'S GUIDE
TO VANQUISHING EVIL

CHRIS BEHRSIN

WORLDWALKERS
PUBLISHING

Copyediting and Proofreading by Tarryn Thomas (www.tarrynthomas.com)
Cover Design Layout by Chris Behrsin

ISBN: 978-1-915886-05-7 (paperback)
ISBN: 978-1-915866-11-8 (hardcover)
ISBN: 978-1-915886-17-0 (e-book)

Published by Worldwalkers Publishing

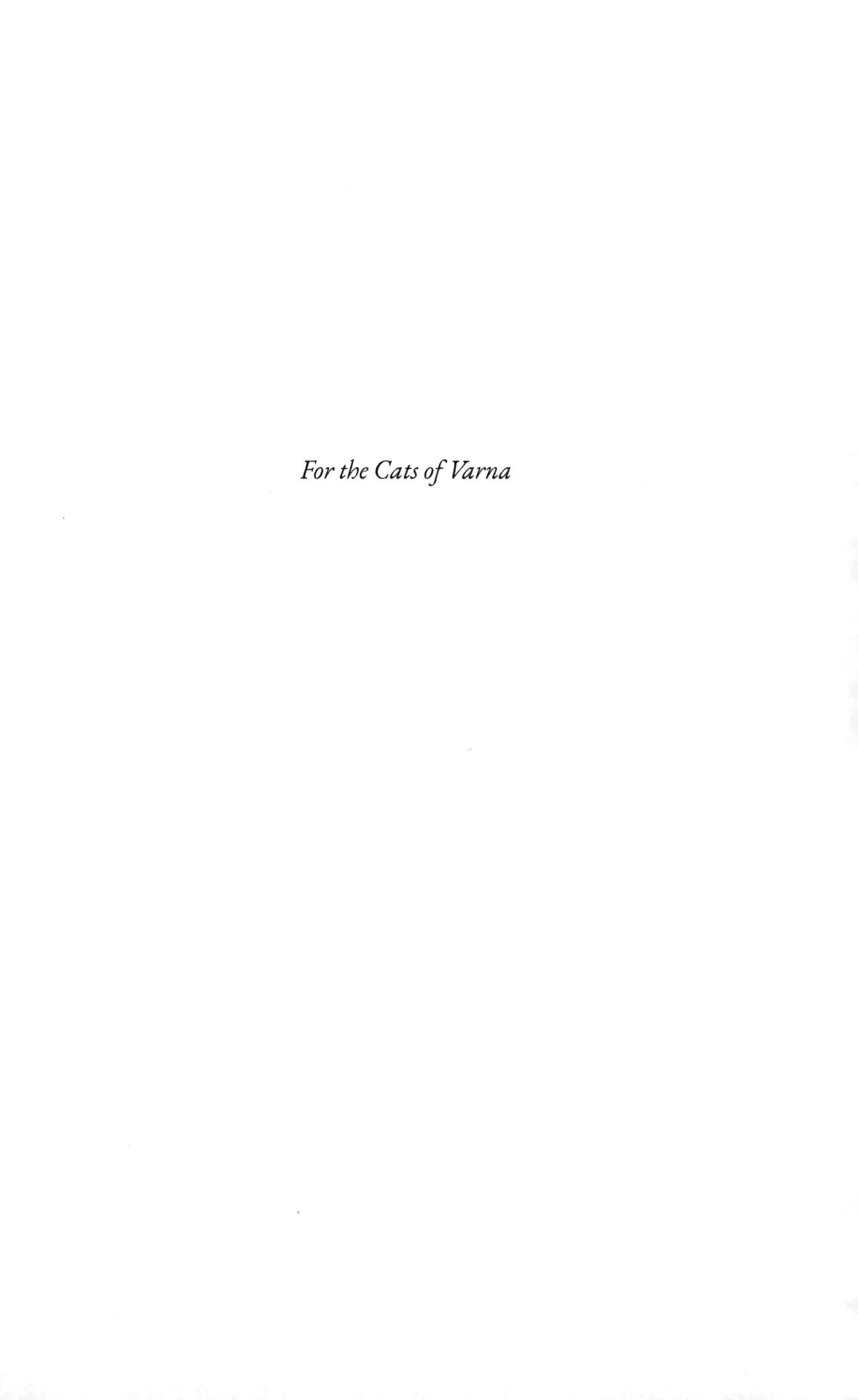

For the Cats of Varna

WHERE IS THE KEY?

Max, the Sussex spaniel who could walk the dimensions, panted innocently as if he had committed no crime.

I watched him for a moment, from my place on the upholstered seat, as our carriage ambled along, rocking over the rough road. It was pulled by four beasts that stank to high heaven of regular horse. The wind howled through the bars that covered the left side window – a bitter chill descending from a leaden sky.

The unicorns weren't pulling the carriage – they wouldn't deign to lower themselves to perform such a task. But they still were part of the White Guard. The White Mages who were currently riding them were casting a spell on this whole carriage and its horses, both keeping everyone invisible and creating a magical annulment field so that no magic could get out or in.

We were too dangerous, Captain Alliander had reasoned. She couldn't trust us to ride on our dragons. Or rather she couldn't trust Seramina, after the young teenager had almost destroyed the worlds. I couldn't blame Alliander for that, admittedly, because I wasn't sure how much I trusted Seramina either.

In fact, I wasn't sure if I could trust anyone here. The only creature I knew I could trust was my dragon, Salanraja, and I was unable to talk to her.

My tail thrashed against the upholstery, and I could sense Esme's stare as she observed me from the opposite seat, her bright blue eyes shining above her pink nose. My Abyssinian companion seemed to have given up interrogating the foolish dog, but I hadn't.

Technically, Esme didn't have to be locked here inside this carriage with us. Because of Esme's skill in white magic and ability to use it alongside the dark, Alliander trusted Esme. It was the white Abyssinian, in fact, who would be training us in the art of the magic that in most cases was channelled through a unicorn's horn. But Esme didn't have a unicorn – she had a dragon – and she was going to teach us exactly where she channelled her magic from.

Still, Esme had to abide by the rules, and her usually invisible staff bearer – in other words the giant, magical white hand that carried her staff for her – had to stay outside.

"It's much safer," Alliander had said, "if magic isn't kept inside a magical containment field."

Perhaps the captain of the White Guard didn't trust Esme quite so much after all. Though I guess it didn't really matter to her – all she seemed to want right now was a good nap.

"I'm going to try again," I whined in the dog language at Max, who had now turned his head towards the opposite window, his floppy ears swaying. "If you don't reveal the location of the Key to the Sixth Dimension, I will scratch at your nose. And I'll make sure it hurts, I tell you."

Max turned back to me and let out an unintelligible growl. "Why won't you shut up, Dragoncat?" he asked, with a softer whimper. "I've told you all I'm going to tell on this subject."

"Because I told Esme that by the time we camp for the night, I'll get it out of you. So talk!"

"Esme said that you have to respect Bastet's wishes. She wants to keep the key hidden."

"How would you know? You can't speak the cat language."

"No, but I can hear Bastet inside my mind, and she tells me exactly what I need to know."

That made me wonder if in fact some magic was working in this place. Perhaps if Bastet, or the crystals that translated her words telepathically, deigned to talk to me, then I'd be able to hear her too. But they didn't – and that left me feeling slightly jealous of Max.

"Esme's asleep," I said, "so she won't be able to chide me for scratching you."

"No, she's not," Max said, turning his head towards her.

"She is. She just likes to sleep with her eyes open sometimes. That way she can see what's happening from inside her dreams."

"You lie," Max barked.

That caused Esme to toss her head upwards. Then she hissed at him for being so loud.

"Stop harassing the dog, Ben," Asinda said. The red-haired prefect of Dragonsbond Academy was one of the human students locked in the carriage with us, the other being Seramina. They sat on either side of Esme. "We all want some peace and quiet."

I let out a low growl, but I said nothing to Asinda. Instead, I looked at Seramina, hoping for some support. Just a few days ago, Seramina had over-channelled the powerful dark force, *Cana Dei*, almost destroying this world and the other dimensions in the process. She could still be under the influence of *Cana Dei*, for all we knew. It was also possible that Arran – or any followers of any warlock or demon for that matter – had posted spies in our convoy.

Seramina saw me looking at her. She shook her head, her long silver hair waving gently from side to side, and looked away, her eyes dull.

Only Esme and I, and our dragons, knew that Max didn't still have the key inside his belly. Oh, and Ange's cheetah Palimali knew also, but she didn't know the human language and so had no way of communicating her knowledge to any human. Besides, Ange wasn't here. She was back in Dragonsbond Academy with her boyfriend, Rine. Despite my dreams of settling down with the two of them after the wars were over, I didn't know if I'd see them ever again.

I turned towards the opposite window, twisting my nose at the stench of horse and unicorn. To meet it seemed preferable to facing Asinda's probing stare.

"Still nothing from him," I said to Salanraja for what must have been the umpteenth time.

But magic includes telepathy, and magic wasn't allowed in this annulment field. So I didn't have the bond with my dragon that I usually had.

I turned my ears towards the window, despite the way they stung in the cold, and listened out for the sign of her wings swishing. She was still there, flying overhead, ready to attack anything that dared assail us. I tried summoning my staff bearer once more, even though I knew it wouldn't work. Eventually I gave myself a headache, and so I returned to a more leisurely activity – in other words, grooming my fur.

I must have got halfway down my shoulder to my chest when I saw a flash of light from the window.

At first I thought it was a massive bluebottle or bee, but it didn't fly like any insect. Rather it moved like a tiny projectile – and landed on the seat right next to me, where it glowed momentarily. Soon the glow faded, however, and the thing vanished into thin air.

I blinked twice, wondering if I was seeing things. I'd heard students say in the past that if someone was kept from their magic for too long, they might start hallucinating.

"Did any of you see that?" I asked. "Esme? Seramina?"

Seramina again shook her head slowly. She had been quiet all journey long – looking both incredibly tired and not smelling as strongly of the snowdrop perfume she used to put on every day. She'd passed her fourteenth birthday a few days ago, but no one had celebrated. It was our first day of travelling within this carriage, and when I'd mentioned her birthday, she had told me to shut up.

Those might well have been the only two words she'd said since she'd channelled *Cana Dei* and forced us all to come to the School of the White.

"Esme?" I asked in the human language.

The Abyssinian opened her eyes and yawned. "Dragoncat, you are so jittery nowadays."

"But I saw it." I said. "Something landed right there beside me. Except it isn't there now."

With a growl, Esme lifted herself up on her haunches, her legs shaking as she stretched. She leaped off her seat and onto mine, and then she sniffed at the leather of the chair.

"Nothing," she said. "Magic withdrawal symptoms, I guess ..."

"But I've hardly ever used magic," I said. "And I didn't just see it, I felt it land, and I heard it go *thwuck* against the chair."

"Then why can't I see or smell anything there?"

"There has to be something." I stalked forward, brushing past Esme and sniffing for the stench of rotten vegetable juice. "It looked like some kind of glowing insect."

"Perhaps a *magefly*," Asinda said. "They live near Cimlean City, and apparently they've learned to draw off its magic. But they don't come out during the day."

Esme looked at Asinda and blinked at her as if she thought she was being stupid. She edged over and curled up beside me. "There, Bengie. Maybe if I sleep close, you'll relax a little."

I did relax, purring deeply. The wind seemed to whisper as it came down from the window, trying to cut through me, but the heat coming out of Esme's body seemed to block it out. I closed my eyes and listened. Something was off.

The seat – it seemed to be vibrating. Behind the sounds of the wind, I could hear another voice developing. It quickly turned into something recognisable, and an unpleasant warmth touched my eyelids. I opened my eyes to see a glow enveloping the space where I thought that the object had landed.

I didn't like the voice I heard next.

It sent the hackles up on the back of my neck. Out of the corner of my eye I saw Seramina, Asinda, and Esme shoot up in their seats. Max growled and snarled, and there came an even brighter flash of light from the same location.

"You know," the voice said. "You should really listen to Dragoncat sometimes."

As if by magic, Arran, the Warlock Prince, had appeared.

AN UNEXPECTED GUEST

Arran sat casually on the seat next to Esme. He looked as if he'd been there for a long time, enjoying the journey. But none of us liked him being there.

Seramina reached over her shoulder reflexively, before realising that her staff wasn't in fact there. Esme closed her eyes as if she were trying to concentrate. But she couldn't summon her staff bearer either. It was stuck somewhere outside the carriage, just like mine.

The difference was that Esme's staff bearer still carried hers, while Captain Alliander had sequestered my, Seramina's, and Asinda's staffs somewhere out of reach.

Which was a shame, because they would have been awfully handy.

Esme stood up on all fours and hissed at Arran with her back arched, showing a full set of impressively sharp feline teeth. Max was also barking away, snarling and growling.

"Magical bad master," he shouted. "Magical bad master. Old master has become evil magical warg."

Somehow, I doubted any of that was going to help. I lazily swept a paw through Arran's flank to confirm that we were indeed looking at an illusion of him.

Asinda's reaction was probably the smartest of all. She stood up, thrust her face to the window opposite the one the object had come in by, and screamed out, "Imposter! We need aid at once!"

Arran turned to look at Asinda, displaying an expression which I didn't recognise in him. Usually he came across as pompous and high and mighty, but now he simply lowered his eyebrows in a slight frown and slowly shook his head. The rest of his face remained expressionless, as if all the muscles of his face had lost the will to move.

His skin was pale, and his eyes were greyer than I'd ever seen them before. Eggshell cracks ran all along his face, blue light shining out beneath them. I caught a whiff of rotten vegetable juice, and I knew immediately that dark magic was involved.

"Captain Alliander!" Asinda screamed at the top of her lungs. "Prince Arran is in here. We need help at once!"

"That's it, young dark mage, waste your breath on pointless undertakings," Arran said in a soft cooing voice. "Alas, this magical annulment field that my dear *stepsister* has cast can be fortified from the inside. They can't hear you, and they won't be able to see you either."

By this point, Esme had calmed down a little. She leaped across the gap between the two carriage seats and started to sniff at Arran, without allowing her nose to pass through the glamour.

"There must be a crystal somewhere, Ben," she said. "Help me work out where it is."

"What are you going to do?" I asked. "Take it in your mouth? Because I did that once with one of Astravar's crystals, and it ended up finding a way into my brain."

"No," Esme said. "We'll throw it out of the window. But first we need to locate it."

"Don't you want to hear what I have to say before you tell me farewell?" Arran asked, and he looked up at Seramina. "For if you get rid of this spell, I can always throw in another crystal."

Seramina nodded her head slowly. "We don't lose anything by letting him speak."

Asinda snapped her head around, and her harsh cornflower-blue stare fell upon the young teenager.

"Seramina, you're not in any position to be giving advice right now. Not after what you did."

"Oh shut up, will you, just for a moment," Seramina said. "I want to hear what he has to say."

"But he's inhabited by *Cana Dei,*" Esme said. "Can't you see it in his eyes?"

"Yes, I do. He's completely lost to it," Seramina said, shaking her head.

"This is why we must find that crystal and throw it out of the window," Esme said.

"No!" Seramina snapped. "If he managed to throw one in, he can throw in another. Why don't we just listen to what he has to say?"

Esme growled quietly but said no more. Asinda turned to face Arran, and even Max stopped barking, instead studying the Warlock Prince with wide and fearful eyes.

"I thought you'd come to your senses," Arran said. "Because you'll most likely find the information I provide will be quite valuable to your convoy. Maybe my dear sister Alliander will even allow you to ride the rest of the journey in the open air. I'm sure you all want to be able to talk to your dragons."

"We can trust nothing that you tell us, Arran," Asinda spat. "You've been a traitor to our cause from the very start."

Arran examined his fingernails. They glowed an eerie purple.

"Whoever this man you knew as Arran was, I am no longer he.

The body you see before you, or at least this image of a body, is now a servant to *Cana Dei*, as are the demon overlords in the Seventh Dimension. But you know all this. One day, you shall all join my cause, and you " Arran pointed a wiry finger at Seramina, a faint purple mist seeming to rise from his fingernails, as if his entire body could control dark magic without the aid of a staff, "—young Seramina, shall be the first to join our cause."

Seramina glared at him.

"Then again," Arran said, turning to me, "maybe not. Maybe we can recruit other allies first."

"Right, that's it," Asinda said, pushing towards Arran, her arm outstretched. Her hand passed right through the Warlock Prince's chest, but then there came a loud boom and she was flung back into her seat by an invisible force. She sat pinned against the seat as if some dark magic was pressing her into it.

Arran's eyes had started to glow bright white, fire burning at the back of them.

"None of you shall be allowed to interfere with the plans of *Cana Dei*. You can only work with us. There is no other way."

"Let her go," Esme said, letting out a long hiss.

"Very well," Arran said, snapping his head around towards Esme. "So long as the red-haired one promises to be compliant."

Asinda meanwhile was writhing in place, trying to escape the invisible spell. Her face was pale, and she looked as if she were struggling to breathe.

"Fine," she said, her voice hoarse.

Arran nodded and Asinda dropped back down to the seat, breathing heavily. Seramina was watching her with a passive gaze. Whiskers, if I found out she'd been a part of this I didn't know what I'd do.

Max continued to bark at Arran, but it didn't seem to perturb the

Warlock Prince one bit. Arran turned his gaze slowly towards the dog. His burning eyes seemed to penetrate so deeply that Max fell silent, clasping his mouth shut. He didn't even seem to want to whimper.

"It's you I came for," Arran said. "Because I've been searching with my pet around Dragonsbond Academy for days, and I can't find the Key to the Sixth Dimension. Where did you put it, dog?"

I laughed at him. I couldn't help myself. It was a habit I'd picked up after days of speaking the human language.

"Is something funny, Dragoncat?"

I meowed as I spoke in the cat language: "It's just that you're asking the one person who doesn't speak your language for information. Looks like you've got no way of getting an answer."

Arran, much to my surprise, responded in my own tongue. "Then it's a good thing *Cana Dei* is universal to all species," he said. "I just wanted to make sure that you all understood exactly what I wanted."

He proceeded to ask the same question that he'd asked in the human language in the dog tongue. It looked quite comical to see a human yip, whine, and bay away like that.

Max didn't look impressed by Arran's multi-lingual abilities. Instead he continued to bark away in a gruff voice.

"You insult me, evil master. You speak my language. But you don't even say hello."

"So, hello, dog. It's nice to finally—"

"It's too late now! You can speak to me in any language you like. It doesn't matter. I've lost all respect for you. You're an ugly, evil warg!"

Max just didn't get it. He called everything a warg except wargs themselves. In fact, I don't think he'd even encountered a real warg yet.

"Humans can't be wargs," I offered.

"Shut up! Get rid of him! I don't know how he got here, but he shouldn't be in this carriage."

Arran didn't even shake his head. Despite Max barking as though he wanted to bite Arran's head off, the Warlock Prince's expression remained profoundly calm.

"I thought it would go like this," Arran said back in the human language. "Very well ... if you won't tell me civilly then I'll discover it through magic."

His skin glowed even brighter, and even more light shone out from those eggshell cracks. Max immediately fell silent again. He stood stock still, paralysed as if he'd been turned to stone for the second time in his life. His eyes bulged in their sockets.

"So that's it ..." Arran said, and his eyes lit up as if he'd discovered something.

"Oh no, you don't," Esme said, and she lunged towards the crystal. She disappeared behind Arran's glamour.

"Esme!" I shouted.

A moment later, she shot out again. Esme leapt to the other seat and deposited a glowing crystal into Asinda's open palm. The red-haired teenager didn't waste a moment in throwing the crystal out of the window.

The world seemed silent for a moment. A sensation of static, which had been coming from the window, seemed to ebb, and it felt as if I could breathe once again. Presently I heard hoofbeats, and then loud voices. Alliander pressed her face up to the bars of the window on Asinda's side.

"What in the Seventh Dimension is going on in here?"

THE CULPRIT

When my master and mistress back in South Wales used to go on holidays, they'd put me in a small plastic cage with tiny slits in the side, and barely enough room between the bars at the front to put a paw through. When we'd finally reached our intended destination – the cattery – every single cat I met there would say the same thing. On that feared day, we'd spend more time hiding under the bed or in the deepest darkest corners of our masters' and mistresses' houses than any other day in the year.

Even though I'd had a lot more space, being cooped up in that carriage had reminded me of the cage a little. Fortunately we didn't have to go back inside. After hearing what had happened in there, Captain Alliander had deemed it better that she keep an eye on us all.

I could smell the wheat in the surrounding fields and taste the freshness of the air. We weren't far from Cimlean City now – its minarets resting lazily upon its gleaming city walls. The flat land-scape rose towards far, rolling hills covered in faint shrouds of slow-moving mist. Cows mooed in the distance and our unicorns and horses whickered in response. Flies buzzed around the horses, only to be swatted away by their lazily swishing tails.

I craned my head up to see my ruby dragon swooping overhead, her arms outstretched. Her shadow passed over me as she glided over to the west. The other dragons were up there too – all six of them together.

"*Ben, it's good to be able to talk to you again,*" Salanraja said in my mind. "*It was so strange being cut off from you like that, knowing that we were still in the same dimension.*"

"*At least this time you know it wasn't my actions that separated us.*"

"*That's debatable,*" Salanraja said.

I knew exactly what she meant. If we hadn't jumped through the portals to stop Arran in his tracks, Seramina might not have been exposed to *Cana Dei* long enough while in the Ghost Realm to unleash the chaos she had caused.

"*You know that we did what we had to do,*" I said. "*Now it sometimes feels like we're being punished for it.*"

"*It's not a punishment, it's a precaution. Even Hallinar's not sure he can trust Seramina anymore. Olan might have kept the old man Aleam from the darkness, but Hallinar's only young and he's not sure he's up to the job.*"

"*We'll find a way to bring back the old Seramina again,*" I said.

Salanraja paused. "*Did Arran discover Max's secret?*"

"*I don't know,*" I said.

"*Perhaps you should tell Captain Alli—*"

"*No,*" I interrupted. "*For all we know, Alliander could have thrown the crystal in herself.*"

"*And why would she have done that?*"

"*Well, she is his half-sister, isn't she?*"

"*Yeah, and she hates him.*"

"It's just that we shouldn't trust anyone yet. So don't tell the other dragons that Max no longer has the key."

"Fine," Salanraja said. *"Just be careful, Ben."*

"I will be."

Alliander stood close to us, beside her unicorn, Tanni. Her lieutenants – Larmend and Carmista – sat nearby, mounted on their own unicorns and keeping watch. My ears latched onto the sound of hoofbeats and I turned my head towards an approaching unicorn.

A male White Mage with a large, hooked nose sat atop it, his cloak whipping behind him as his mount trotted towards us. A guard in shiny chainmail lay slumped across the unicorn's back.

The unicorn walked up to Alliander and the mage dismounted. He saluted Captain Alliander then turned towards the man.

"Your report, Plagis," Alliander said.

"I think this is our culprit, Ma'am," Plagis replied. "He attacked me, so I cast a spell to knock him out cold."

Alliander nodded, and pulled up the guard's head by his stringy hair. She used a white-gloved hand to open his eyes and examine them. "How did he do it?"

Plagis reached into the pocket at the front of his robe and produced a grey pouch, tied at the top with a rough hemp drawstring. A metal pipe was sticking out of the top which he lifted out between two fingers.

"Blowpipe, Ma'am. Must have quite a huff to him."

"Magically augmented, no doubt," Alliander said, and she reached for the pouch.

From it she produced a crystal just like the one that had landed next to me, and I could tell there were more where that came from. As soon as she held it up to the light, it glowed faintly and disintegrated into dust, and was carried away upon the breeze.

Alliander looked at Carmista, then at Larmend.

"We must be vigilant," she said. "Arran might have agents anywhere in Cimlean City – the greater the population, the greater their chances. Larmend, take two White Guards and conduct a thorough search of the school. Put it on lockdown until it's completed."

Larmend saluted. "Yes, Ma'am."

At a nod from Alliander, he trotted off. He took two mounted White Guards with him as ordered, but there were so many White Guards with us that I doubted we'd notice any change in numbers. Soon the three unicorns kicked back their legs and galloped into the distance, throwing up tufts of grass behind them.

Alliander watched them go, and then spoke to her other lieutenant.

"Carmista, take this guard to the barracks and lock him in the dungeons. We'll question him later and see if we can heal him. Plagis can go with you, too."

Carmista saluted and mounted her unicorn. At a much more careful pace, she and Plagis – with the guard still lying across his mount – cantered off towards the east side of the city.

"What about the rest of us?" Asinda asked Alliander. She had her hands on her hips. "You're not going to lock us up in the carriage again after all that, are you?"

"Certainly not." Alliander scowled, clearly not liking being spoken to in that tone. Asinda had been talking down to Alliander ever since the captain had forced her to separate from her boyfriend, Lars. "No more glamours; no more tricks. It's only another ten miles to the school now."

"So does that mean we can take our dragons?" Asinda asked.

"No," Alliander said. "As I've already stated, I need you all where I can keep an eye on you."

She nodded towards the horses – one piebald, one bay, and two duns – who were still harnessed to the carriage, munching happily on the grass. "Have any of you been trained to ride bareback?"

"Can't say I have," Asinda said, and glanced at Seramina.

Seramina shook her head, saying nothing. Max also remained quiet, for obvious reasons. Esme, like myself, also didn't utter a word. I guess she was thinking the same thing I was – there was no way we were getting on a horse.

Alliander nodded, as if she'd expected it. "Then you'd better be able to move your legs at a good pace, because we're going to have to march."

❧ 4 ❧

SNUBBED

If there is one thing in all the dimensions that cats aren't designed for, it's walking long distances. The old Ragamuffin back home in South Wales had told us that in a faraway land on the other side of a vast ocean, humans would put harnesses on cats and take them out for a stroll in the park. Humans in the Fourth Dimension did something similar with dogs, apparently – they put a rope around their necks and strangled them if they tried to veer off course.

From the way that Alliander watched us from Tanni's back, I had no doubt that if Max or I had decided to go for a wander, she'd try the same on us. Whiskers, she might even do it to Asinda or Seramina, knowing her. Once again it seemed that only Esme was safe. Although I doubted she much liked marching either.

We trooped along a dusty dirt track, which I didn't like because I kept getting grit in the gaps between the pads of my paws. Mounted unicorns marched on all sides of us, with Alliander and Tanni on our right. Their White Guard riders all kept their gnarled

⤙ 18 ⤚

oaken staffs in their hands, ready no doubt to cast a spell if any of us made one false move.

As we approached Cimlean City, signs of human civilisation became more prevalent. The dirt track started to show bits of stone in it. At first they looked as if they'd tumbled across the path by accident, but they soon became shiny-looking cobblestones.

The fields and meadows slowly became huts and hovels, and the cows were replaced by humans and their businesses. Heat blared out from the workshops of blacksmiths and farriers. The scent of milled flour and baked bread wafted over, replacing the natural scents of pollen. The insects buzzed less and the sounds of industry roared more.

Surprisingly, I also saw more cats in the villages that clung to Cimlean City's walls. Given how things were in Dragonsbond Academy, I had expected them to also be locked in a cattery, only let out at night to hunt rats and mice. I commented upon this to Esme.

"You would have thought that place was a prison, the way you grumble about it," she replied, her head held high as she strolled. While my legs were tired from marching for miles and I felt myself wanting to lag behind, she seemed to be keeping the pace quite well.

"Isn't it?" I asked. "Cats shouldn't be locked up indoors, and I don't care if it's during the day or night. They should be allowed to roam outside for as long as they please."

"It's actually quite a nice place. The cats enjoy it in there. They're not locked in cages as in those catteries that you've told me about, and there are plenty of spaces for them to roam about, plenty of toys to play with, and more food than any cat could possibly need. I found it quite pleasant while I was there."

I growled. It didn't matter how much space they had inside there. She made it sound just like the catteries that I used to go on holiday in. A cat should never be removed from their territory.

"I can't imagine I'd enjoy it," I said.

"And did you ever visit to check it out?" Esme asked.

"No ..."

"Then did you talk to any of the other cats about what they thought about their lodgings?"

"Can't say I did," I said.

Esme let out an amused chirp. "No wonder the other cats back at Dragonsbond Academy think you're a snob."

"You what?"

"A snob. They say that because you're from another world and can use magic, you think you're better than them."

"I don't."

"Their words, not mine. But it's true, isn't it? You're much more likely to rub shoulders with dragons and humans than your own kind."

"That's how it's always been," I said. "So long as humans put food in our bowls."

"Has it?" Esme said, looking at me with a cock of her head.

I had nothing to say in response, because I knew that Esme spoke the truth. Even though I was becoming less reliant on the humans and more independent, I was also becoming more human and losing my catness. For a while I'd thought I was proud of that. But my time spent with Esme had made me realise I had started to forget who I was.

Seramina had also forgotten who she was for a while – and *Cana Dei* had taken advantage of that and used her as a receptacle to try to destroy the dimensions. Sometimes I feared that the same might happen to me.

Esme didn't study me for long before she marched onwards to converse with Max in the dog language. I let her carry on ahead. She didn't seem to want to get as close to me as she used to.

I guessed she'd decided I was no longer worth her time.

AN UNFAMILIAR VOICE

As we got closer to the city, the walls seemed to shine more brightly. At first I thought this was just the sun reflecting off a coat of brilliant white paint – but they weren't just reflecting the light, they were emitting it. They also let out the kind of heat that made me want to curl up beside them and go to sleep.

I guess it had been an awfully long journey. If you'd asked me what things a cat shouldn't be deprived of, other than its territory, I'd have put a good nap pretty high on the list.

Asinda caught me slowing down to gaze at it. "They post White Mages and unicorns at the bottom of each of the towers," she said.

She was walking on one side of me now, Seramina on the other. "Droves of young graduates of the School of the White work long shifts to keep the magic flowing."

"Why? What does the magic do?"

"It's not about what it does, but what it controls. It stops certain kinds of magic being used in the city. They say you can't cast dark magic here, and it's also why it's impossible to summon a portal inside the walls."

"You know a lot about it," I said.

Asinda smirked. It was good to see her forget about missing Lars, at least for the moment. "I was born into royalty. Throughout my childhood, there was always someone telling me how the city works."

Come to think of it, when I squinted my eyes I could just about make out the fields of magic pulsing through the defences. I wondered if I would have been able to do this before I'd become a mage, or if it was one of the benefits of the job.

I perked up my ears and listened to the towers thrumming in a low frequency, sending off a soothing resonance. As I studied the ebb and flow of the magic, I noticed how it seemed to originate from one tower at the centre of it all. It was perhaps the tallest tower I'd ever seen, much taller than Astravar's tower had been. Taller even than the Keep Tower at Dragonsbond Academy.

"What about the largest of the towers?" I asked. "Is it special in some way?"

Asinda nodded. "That's the Tower of the Grand. Much of the magic of the city is sourced from there."

"So there must be a lot of unicorns in there," I said, turning up my nose at the thought of them.

"No, the unicorns guard the courtyard. But there's just a few White Mages and the King's Crystal inside."

"I've heard of that. It's like the Great Crystal in Dragonsbond Academy, right?"

"Except it's much bigger," Asinda said. "The King's Crystal is the greatest source of magic known inside this realm."

I was purring, getting all excited just thinking about it. Maybe if I could draw off its power, I could finally complete my dream of bringing salmon into this dimension.

Just as I had become lost in that thought, my mouth watering as I imagined the delicious breakfasts I could be eating, time suddenly seemed to slow around me. The air seemed to thin, and for a while I thought I saw purple mist rising from the city walls.

But I wasn't afraid. Nothing could scare me now ...

You can have it all, an unfamiliar voice said in my head. *Join us, Dragoncat. Claim what is your right.*

The voice sounded so enticing, even more so than the lilting Welsh-sounding voice of my crystal. I wanted to bring it closer – to listen to it forever.

But when I tried to focus on it, it had vanished from my mind.

THE SCHOOL OF THE WHITE

I reached the School of the White with every single muscle in my body aching.

My legs, my shoulders, my spine. Everything felt as if it had needles sticking out of it. By this time the sun had already set and twilight had spread, filling the sky with a deep velvety texture.

The academy was built into the city, the walls jutting out at slight angles to support an octagonal complex. It had parapets and towers of its own, which made it like a mini castle among the other buildings. The whole structure glowed white, the same as the city walls. From every inch of the shining mortar came a loud humming sound. It reminded me of the substation that powered my home village back in South Wales – the one that every single cat knew instinctively to avoid at all costs, and certainly to not try climbing its metal struts.

The unicorns drew up next to a tall pair of closed doors, with a large white crystal set into the wood between them at the centre. Alliander took Tanni to the front of our formation. She used her staff to cast a beam of white magic into the centre of the crystal.

After that, the doors seemed to open of their own accord.

Night had settled quickly, and we didn't see much of the academy or the students who studied at the School of the White. Our convoy soon dissipated into the stone buildings that jutted out from the wall. Our dragons also left us there, flying over to the Dragon Barracks on the north side of the city. We could talk to them inside the School of the White, but we could only see them twice a week during 'dragon visiting hours'.

Salanraja didn't seem to want to talk to me much, though. She seemed more interested in meeting some famous dragons of the Dragon Guard. I was starting to feel a little cut off.

The unicorns and humans seemed to share the same quarters. Honestly, the white mages seemed to treat their unicorns like cats were treated back home.

Though there was a chill in the air, the warmth coming from the walls alleviated it somewhat.

I wondered if you could cook meat on the walls too, because I really fancied a mutton sausage. All through the journey, we'd had to eat processed cat food while the humans had been stuck with rice and courgettes, with only a little meat thrown in. I knew times were hard and all that, but I'd seen plenty of cows in the fields we'd passed. At the very least the humans could have afforded us a bowl of milk.

Only Alliander and a couple of White Guards remained to lead us to our quarters. We went on foot – the unicorns seeming to want to settle in for the night, also tired from the long march. We followed the robed mages towards a wooden, red-painted barn at the edge of the complex that stank of horse.

"You've got to be kidding," I moaned. "Out of all the cosy places you have, you're putting us up in the stable?"

Alliander bowed her head. "I'm sorry, but all the beds are taken this year. We've done what we can to make your accommodations comfortable."

"So in other words, the unicorns have had an upgrade," I said.

I tilted my head to indicate the stone buildings. The glow coming from their walls made them feel lovely and warm.

Alliander chuckled. "This is the stable for the regular horses of any visitors who aren't white mages or dragon riders. Unicorns would never stay in a barn like this."

"Great," I muttered, and went through the entrance that didn't have any doors to close against the wind. Hopefully the magic from the walls outside the barn would keep us warm, but there was a definite chill.

"Enjoy," Alliander said, and left us alone.

Alliander posted two White Guards outside our door, and they could easily watch us as we slept to ensure that we didn't get up to anything. There were a couple of beds with mattresses at the end, one each for Seramina and Asinda. For Esme and me, two wicker baskets hung from a rafter on the ceiling, stuffed with straw. Max also had a basket, but his had been placed on the floor.

None of us intended to use the baskets, though. Esme and I slept curled up on either side of Asinda, while Max occupied half of Seramina's bed. The mattresses weren't quite the softest, but we all slept well that night, exhausted from the day's march.

NOT QUITE A FEAST

A rooster woke us up at dawn the next day and it wouldn't shut up, even when I went outside and hissed at it. The white fluffy bird turned its head towards me, its yellow eyes blinking underneath its red crest. I hissed again, but it didn't move from its spot and it didn't stop crowing.

The Savannah cats back in South Wales had told me never to mess with roosters – they are much more vicious than they look. So I decided to leave it alone, instead following the smell of food wafting out of a nearby building that stood next to a tower with a shining bell on top. The food didn't smell like courgettes, but like salty roast pork.

As soon as I recognised the scent, I lost control of my legs. They took me to where my stomach wanted them to go.

Max and Esme weren't far behind me, clearly latching on to the scent as well. We reached the door, and a male White Guard with a beard awaited us there. He looked down at the three of us with deep, cavernous eyes. He had his staff clutched in his hand and the crystals along its length were glowing so brightly that I knew he would cast a spell to block our passage.

I miaowed, trying to behave like the cutest Bengal in the world. This didn't soften the man's features in any way. Perhaps Esme was right – I was losing my touch. Humans, or those that behaved like them, had much more trouble getting their own way than cats did.

"We are here for breakfast," Esme said, opting instead to use the human language over the cute feline one.

"Say what?" the guard said.

"Breakfast," I said. "In other words, what you're serving in there."

"Smell great! Smells great!" Max barked. "I'm the hungriest dog ever!"

The guard shrugged. "I know what breakfast is. I just wasn't told that we'd have talking cats eating with us."

"And a dog," Esme said.

The guard looked down at Max. "Yes, and a dog ... I mean, I knew that there would be animals. I just didn't know that you'd talk. I was told we were meant to put down your food in bowls."

I let out a deep growl. Max joined in for effect.

"We're not eating any more of that pig's intestine swill," I said. "We want the real deal. Good roast pork like you're cooking in there."

"I thought you were supposed to be with two humans. Two young ladies, I heard. Both very powerful *magicians*."

He coughed against the back of his hand.

I looked at Esme. "On all the days they choose to lie in," I said, still in the human language. "I guess we're going to have to wake them."

But I was in luck, because I heard female footsteps approaching and caught a whiff of Seramina's snowdrop perfume. Both dark mage students walked towards us, with their hair messed up and massive bags under their eyes.

"We would have slept longer," Asinda said, with a yawn. "But the smell woke us. I thought we'd have to eat vegetables and rice for months."

"You're in luck," the guard said with a clearly fake smile. "This is a special feast to welcome the new students, which I guess would be you. Really, the School of the White would create any excuse for a good breakfast. Particularly in such hard times."

He stepped aside.

We entered the dining hall, which wasn't too different to the one at Dragonsbond Academy. Long wooden tables stretched across the length of a hall, lit by tall tallow candles burning in gigantic chandeliers hanging from the ceiling. Students in white robes sat along the tables, each next to their unicorns. I couldn't see the food, but I could smell it. Both the students and the unicorns were happily munching on plates of roast pork, gravy, and mashed potatoes.

"Unicorns will eat anything," Alliander had told me once, and I could now see she was right.

We stepped forwards. The chatter in the room ground to a halt, and everyone in the hall turned their heads to stare at us. They definitely looked like they didn't want us to be here. We weren't welcome.

The guard who'd been waiting at the door had followed us into the room.

"I was meant to show you all to your table, I think," he said. "You're not to eat with the regulars."

He led us over to a white paper screen, with a blue floral design painted on it. Behind the screen was a small table with seats, set for two. Two plates of food were up there, which smelled delicious. I probably would have leaped onto the table if the guard hadn't been clutching his staff with such a menacing look. Clearly those plates weren't meant for us, as three bowls of what smelled like rancid processed food lay on the floor.

"You weren't kidding." Esme said, looking at the bowls. "I'm meant to be a teacher here. You would have thought that at least I would get some special treatment."

"Yeah, but you're still a cat," the guard replied. "And cats eat what cats eat."

He left us there. Max, Esme, and I went over to examine the bowls. I sniffed them. It was even worse than what Alliander had fed me during the journey.

"There's no way I'm touching that," I said.

"Me neither," Esme said. "I'd rather starve."

That seemed good with Max, because he ended up wolfing down all three bowls.

"Maybe we need to go out and hunt tonight, Ben," Esme said. "We might find a few mice here."

"That's if they've not already been zapped by the white magic running through the walls. Whiskers, what is wrong with these White Mages? I mean, why do they seem to hate cats so much?"

"Because they only care about their unicorns," Esme said. "When I finally get a chance to meet King Garmin, I'll be having a word with him about this. They're meant to have respect for all animals. It's part of their *code*."

Suddenly, a strip of pork fell down from the table. It smelled a lot drier than what I'd sensed on the plates of the regular students, but it was still meat. Esme was much faster in leaping upon it than I was, though. Before I knew it, she was across the room with the meat in her mouth, guarding it with her life.

Seramina had thrown down the meat, and so I looked up at her, made my eyes wide and meowed. I couldn't express how hungry I was. She could probably hear my tummy as much as I could.

A trace of a smile spread across Seramina's lips, and down came another strip of pork. This time it hadn't come from Seramina, but from Asinda. I pounced before it hit the ground and Esme or Max could take an interest in it. I caught it between my paws and carried it in my mouth over to my own private corner.

I ate, feeling rather let down by Alliander and her company. Fortunately my dragon rider companions still cared about us. Perhaps, after Esme had trained us little, the White Mages would change their minds about us, too. But somehow I doubted it.

WHITE MAGIC 101

The bell rang shortly after we'd eaten, my tummy satisfied from the generous servings that Asinda and Seramina had thrown down from their table. We listened to the students file out for a moment, my ears latching on to their impressions of what they thought of us dark mages.

"I heard they might ruin the school with their magic," one student said.

"Rumour has it that the blonde one destroyed the Altar of Lore, almost bringing down both her enemies and her allies in the process."

"I've heard she's Astravar's daughter," another said. "She's dangerous, that one."

Not wanting to listen to any more of this nonsense, I turned my ears towards a couple of girls who were instead talking about Asinda.

"The way that redhead stares ... it's just not natural."

"She hurt her boyfriend, the High Prefect of Dragonsbond Academy, with her magic. That's why they broke up."

"Yeah, she's even more scary than that one with the silver hair. Who knows why they made her a prefect."

Whiskers, it was good they were too far away for Asinda to hear, because she'd be storming over with her fists raised and having words. Esme had her ears turned in the same direction as mine, and she also seemed to think it was better to remain silent.

We waited for all the students to leave. Once the room was empty, Esme strode out from behind the screen. We all followed.

"Alliander told me that we should use the dining room for training," Esme said.

"And how are we meant to do anything without our staffs?" Asinda asked.

She was answered by the click-clack of heels as Alliander strode into the room. Several White Guards – not students – accompanied her, all of them mounted on their unicorns, with their staffs drawn. Alliander had our staffs with her, bundled up in a sheet. Seeing them caused my heart to skip in my chest. Though I knew dark magic was bad for me, I'd missed my staff. I'd missed the ability to summon my staff bearer out of thin air and place it in my mouth, magic ready. It somehow made me feel safe – even if I wasn't particularly powerful as a dark mage.

"Do we really need the guards?" Esme asked, as Alliander approached.

"They're not for you personally, Esme," Alliander said. "They're for when I decide to allow the students to use their staffs."

"And when will that be?" Asinda asked, her gaze fixed on the bundle.

Her fingers twitched as if she wanted to reach out and snatch her staff. Seramina, on the other hand, stared fearfully at the staffs with her eyes wide.

"When I decide," Alliander snapped back. "Now, Esme, proceed with the lesson—" she paused to take a breath "—if you please."

Esme bared her teeth and let out an incredibly quiet hiss. She summoned her staff bearer.

"Very well," she said.

Within an instant, she had her staff clenched in her jaws, every crystal glowing across the length of the gnarled wood. A ball emerged at the tip of it and floated towards the centre of the room. It grew to around the height of a full-grown man, hovering several feet above the floor.

The spell felt warm, just like the walls. It made me wonder why White Mages bothered to build campfires. The air tasted so pure. Flares of white leapt out of and dived back into the surface of the ball like miniature, magical salmon.

Alliander, who stood watching the display with the bundle of staffs now folded against her waist, gave an approving nod.

Though this lesson probably wasn't intended for Max, he had his eyes fixed on the orb, and was panting out in the dog language, "Such beauty! Such beauty!" over and over again.

"This is white magic in its purest form," Esme said. "The essence of creation, a spell that does nothing except warm the surroundings and display its magnificence. Now, I ask you – what do you see within the orb?"

I traced some more dancing salmon with my eyes. "I see tiny magical fish," I said.

"They're not fish," Esme said. "Asinda, would you like to try?"

She shook her head, her arms folded against her chest. "Not particularly," she said. "It's just a ball of white."

"If you don't try," Esme said, "then you won't be able to graduate from this school. How about you, Seramina?"

Seramina was watching the ball with rapt attention. Her eyes looked glazed, but I saw no fire behind them as I did whenever she'd started to lose control.

"I see *Cana Dei*," she said. "Underneath the light."

Asinda snorted. "You would."

"Asinda," Esme said. "You really need to work on your attitude."

Asinda looked away, and Esme didn't press the matter.

"You are perfectly correct, Seramina," Esme said. "There is *Cana Dei* underneath the white magic. *Cana Dei* is a dark destructive force, and white magic gets its power from destroying it. But the only way to destroy destruction is through creation – which is how I learned to abandon dark magic and become a White Mage."

Interest registered on Asinda's face. When I squinted my eyes, I saw that the streaks of light that dived out of and back into the ball weren't in fact created by light at all. They were just an illusion covering up streaks of darkness.

Dragoncat, a voice said in my head. It was the same voice that had reached out to me before. *We can make your life richer.*

I opened my eyes again, wondering where the whiskers that voice could have come from.

Esme turned to me and narrowed her eyes. "Is something the matter, Ben?"

"I ... no, nothing," I said.

I looked up at Alliander, who was watching me with concern.

"Let me get something straight," Asinda said. "You're saying that in order to use white magic, we need to summon the force that we were meant to avoid all along."

She folded her arms.

Esme turned back to her. "Not summon – more like burn."

"Does that mean we could use white magic to destroy *Cana Dei*?" Seramina asked.

"That would take an awful lot of white magic," Esme said. "And *Cana Dei* replenishes fast."

Reach out, Dragoncat, the voice said again. It was so alluring, but it was also incredibly dry. *All that you desire is within your reach, forever. Forget about the light. The darkness can be yours to control.*

Whiskers, I wasn't liking this at all. But at the same time I wanted to hear more. The way that the dark specks danced across the surface of the orb had me mesmerised. I moved my head from side to side as I watched them. Then I started growling.

"Ben," Esme said again. "Do you have anything to add? You're acting rather odd."

Esme's smooth voice pulled me out of the trance. It felt like awakening from a deep and disturbing dream.

"I've got a bad tummy," I said. "I think it must be that pork."

9

STAFFS

The rest of the day was taken up by Esme showing us more displays of white magic. She used a spell to summon a miniature phoenix in the centre of the room, explaining how she sourced the magic as she did so. Like us, she had a crystal in this realm that gifted her with magic, and she only needed to use that crystal to summon dark magic and convert it to light. Unicorns could do this conversion automatically with their horns, but we didn't have unicorns and so we had to work harder to access our magic.

Honestly, I had a sense that Esme was hiding something. We couldn't source our white magic from unicorns, and we couldn't source our white magic from dragons. It just intuitively made sense that we needed to get it from some other creature. I just didn't have a clue from which one.

Esme proceeded to show us more possibilities of what we could do – summoning the spirits of dragons from the Ghost Realm to fight our battles; casting beams of light that could sear through stone, much as dark magic could; creating a magical spy-ball and it's duplicate that could show us exactly what was happening, without sound, in the next room.

I heard no more of that strange voice in my head, and I put it down to tiredness. Whatever it had been, it seemed to have lost interest – at least for the time being.

All through the training Alliander stood by the door, studying each of us without saying a word. She had placed the bundle of staffs next to the guards who stood there. None of us even looked at our staffs. We were all too interested in these magical spells, and what we could do with them. Even Seramina – who was apparently destined to be the most powerful warlock ever – seemed to be learning new things.

We had snacks brought to us throughout the day, so we didn't go hungry. They even put some of that pork in each of our bowls. This time it didn't affect my tummy.

Time flowed like milk from a carton, and night soon befell us. The walls continued to buzz and emit a pleasant warmth that seemed to regulate the temperature of the air in the city. It was hard to hear anything behind it, but I heard – or at least I imagined I heard – the hoot of an owl from outside.

As soon as Esme had finished speaking, Alliander took the opportunity to pick up the bundle of staffs from the floor and hold them out in her arms.

"Tomorrow, you will have an opportunity to cast some spells of your own," she said. "But first, I need to test your resolve. Keep these staffs on your person without reaching for them tonight, and I will know if you use them."

I remembered what Asinda had told me about the walls detecting and regulating what magic was cast within this city. If we did something out of the ordinary, Alliander would almost certainly find out.

Alliander handed Asinda her staff first. The teenager gave a grunt, which I guessed was her way of saying, "I would say thank you, but you had no cause to confiscate my staff in the first place."

Seramina took her staff with a little more gratitude. But she held it only very briefly, before sliding it into the straps on her back as quickly as she could. "I'll do no harm with this, Captain Alliander, I promise," she said, without making eye contact.

Alliander nodded at her with much more confidence than I'd expected, and then she turned to me with a wary gaze. "Dragoncat, summon your staff bearer."

I did as she said. With a flash of light, the gigantic white hand appeared out of nothingness. It made an 'okay' sign, and I willed it forwards. Alliander looked at it, then turned her mistrusting gaze back to me.

"Remember, Dragoncat, no dark magic," she said. "Not even a beam to hunt some mice."

I growled. "Why aren't you saying this to the other two?"

"Let's call it a hunch. Now, I need your word."

"Fine, no dark magic. I won't even summon my staff bearer."

"Good," Alliander said, and she placed my staff in my bearer's palm. Power immediately surged through my muscles. I hadn't realised how weak I'd been feeling. It was as if I were in the process of wolfing down a bowl of tuna after not having eaten for days.

You can use this, Dragoncat, the voice said again in my head.

Shut up, shut up, shut up! I don't want to listen to you.

You cannot shut me off. I am part of you now.

Then I heard another voice. *"Ben,"* it was Salanraja. *"Ben, I finally reached you. Why have you been you cutting me off?"*

"I haven't," I said. *"You've been ignoring me. I know you want to spend some time with your friends, but you could have least said hello. Salanraja, are you listening to me?"*

I waited for a response, but Salanraja didn't seem to be there.

I clenched my jaw to stop myself from growling. I didn't want to draw attention to myself; instead, I turned to Max, who was looking at me wide-eyed. He took a few sniffs at me, keeping his distance.

"You smell funny, Dragoncat," he whined in the dog language. "Like bad cucumber."

This time I did growl, but in a particularly dog-like way. "At least I don't smell like dog," I said.

I turned away as I willed my staff bearer to carry my staff back into the void.

10

AN UNEXPECTED ATTACK

I opted to sleep in the basket that night rather than in Asinda's or Seramina's bed. I'd decided that enough heat came from the walls of the complex outside – even through the insulation of this barn – that I didn't really need extra body heat. Besides, I was worried about the voice that had kept creeping into my head.

I was speaking to *Cana Dei*, I was sure of it. The stuff was meant to consume you. Whiskers, it almost had with Seramina. When she'd channelled it back at the Altar of Lore, she'd managed to draw out so much of it that she'd almost destroyed us all.

The voice didn't visit me again before I fell asleep that night. I drifted off, curled up warmly on the surprisingly soft blanket that the White Mages had put in the wicker basket. Maybe they cared more about cats than I'd actually realised.

In sleep, I revisited a familiar theme.

Bubbles revolved around me, buoying me away from the riverbed, speeding me towards my destination. My scaled skin was sleek against the water. My school shone silver in the sunlight that found its way beneath the surface. Together we sailed over the rapids; together we hurtled towards our destination. Following the currents through the essence of destiny itself, carrying us to where we were meant to go. The only movement I needed was a slow and regular swish of my tail.

I wasn't a cat here, but a salmon, as I had been in many of my dreams. And I was no longer in the First Dimension. Rather, I was travelling the rivers between worlds, using the mechanism of dreams to traverse the pathways that linked the dimensions, which were only accessible through the astral planes.

On my skin, and through the earholes at the side of my head, I could hear the roar approaching – a waterfall which we soon would have to leap. Those who weren't strong enough wouldn't survive. But I would, because I was the mightiest of us all.

I steadied my tail and prepared. I only needed a moment to complete the leap. I performed the necessary motion to gain speed.

Swish, swash, swish, swash.

I tensed every muscle in my body, and I leaped. Rushing through the water, breaking the surface, the spray pushed back against me like the wildest storm. But my leap was sure, and I entered a dark cave mouth, only to land on a red surface, writhing and thudding my tail against the ground.

I was greeted by searing heat coming from all directions. Fish didn't belong out of water, and they certainly didn't belong here.

Must wake up, must wake up.

But there was another voice – cold, dry, yet still reassuring.

Believe in this, Dragoncat. We will work together, and we will unite the seven realms.

The voice brought me back to my mind again, mesmerised. I wasn't a fish anymore, but a cat – a Bengal, descendant of the great Asian leopard cat, the mightiest beast in all the realms.

I was in the Seventh Dimension – the eggy stench of brimstone told me that, enough to recognise it before I even opened my eyes.

My eyelids parted, and I looked up into familiar blue eyes, fires burning behind them. I saw his face then, the features gaunt, eggshell-like cracks lining the surface of his skin.

Arran.

My heart pounded in my chest, the hackles shooting up on my back. This wasn't right—

Must wake up, must wake up, must wake up.

"Relax, Dragoncat," Arran said, his voice slow and measured. "We are all as one here. We are all servants of *Cana Dei*."

"No! Release me from ..." I found my voice drifting away. Something else was starting to replace my thoughts – something enticing, something that I yearned for. A sense of belonging.

I was a part of something important. We were all a part of it – me, Arran, all the demons I could sense across the realm. The other warlocks, if they chose to join us. Other dark mages in Cimlean city, and in the other towns of Illumine Kingdom, who also served *Cana Dei*. Our merged minds could achieve more than humanity had ever imagined.

We could live forever; our memories would never be lost. The whole of civilisation, distilled into an essence of greatness – I could be part of the biggest revolution known to history.

And I could have all the salmon in all the realms to myself.

"What do you ask of me, Arran?" I asked. "What does *Cana Dei* need?"

I had my staff in my mouth, the crystal on it glowing purple. Warmth thrummed through my muscles, and all around me I could smell the sweet scent of dark magic.

Arran raised his head and his eyes focused on something distant. His lips moved of their own accord.

"Summon Bastet, Dragoncat. Summon her here and we can bring retribution upon her for what she did to Apopis."

Another creature loomed close to him. It had two elongated

jaws, each with two rows of sharp, curled teeth. Paws with claws as long as a lion's, and the fattest rear legs I'd ever seen on any creature. She had massive scales all along the length of her body. The cracks between them glowed like the magma sea that surrounded us.

Head of a crocodile, body of a lion, hindquarters of a hippopotamus. I was standing before Ammit herself.

"Can't you summon Bastet?" I asked. "What do you need her for?"

The realisation was coming back to me, my mind fighting to regain its dominion. I didn't belong here. I needed to wake up.

Just think of what we could achieve together, the voice of *Cana Dei* said in my head. *All the smoked salmon you could ever want ...*

Yes, I thought. *This is what I want.* The crystal on my staff glowed white for a second, then purple.

Arran had been watching me wordlessly as I struggled with myself. Once *Cana Dei* had secured its hold on me again, he said, "Bastet promised you that if you summoned her she would come, did she not? Beings of her ilk must honour such promises. Now bring her here."

He was right; Bastet needed to be here. I needed to do my duty so that we could all move together to the next stage. I didn't need to understand what the next stage was – I just had to do what *Cana Dei* needed.

I willed the power to my staff, focusing on a point on the ground. A tiny hole emerged there – a link to the Fifth Dimension.

Suddenly I saw something slither across the terrain, crossing the corner of my vision. I turned to see a long and thin pathetic-looking worm, finding its way across the ground.

Apopis ...

And I remembered ...

The battle back at the Altar of Lore.

How, while Seramina had been summoning *Cana Dei*, Apopis had also entered the scene, attacking anything that moved.

I'd summoned Bastet onto the scene to defeat the demon snake.

Bastet was my friend, and we needed her. If I brought her here, they'd destroy us. They'd destroy us all ...

"No!" I screamed, and I let the energy drain from my staff. "I shall not do it. I do not serve *Cana Dei.*"

Arran's eyes narrowed. He reached behind his back for his staff.

Must wake up. Must wake up. Must wake up.

Something was happening – I wasn't in the Seventh Dimension anymore. Instead, I was swimming the rivers that connected the worlds. I was a salmon again, plummeting down the waterfall.

Come back! You must serve us, Dragoncat.

The voice thinned as I progressed, fighting against the rapids. Doing everything I could to escape.

I broke the surface of the water, and my eyes shot open. I didn't waste a moment springing out of the basket onto my feet to make sure I wouldn't drift off again. Behind me there came the soft snores of cat, humans, and dog, sleeping soundly.

Whatever bad deeds I might have performed, I hadn't woken them. Maybe this had all been a dream.

But I had the staff in my mouth, the crystal at the end of it glowing a faint purple. At the doorway across the room, Alliander stood with her staff clutched in her fist, her gaze focused directly on me.

11

FAREWELL STAFF BEARER

It didn't take Alliander long to rouse Esme, Seramina, and Asinda. The captain of the White Guard only had to clap her hands and their eyes snapped open in an instant. Soon enough, more White Mages flooded into the room, their staffs drawn.

Esme was up on her haunches, yowling at the top of her voice. Seramina and Asinda sprang out of bed too, probably wondering what all the commotion was about. Only Max failed to wake, somehow sleeping through all of it. That didn't matter, because the dog didn't have a staff and so no one cared about him.

Soon, we all stood gathered at the centre of the former stable. Asinda, Seramina, and I stood in a row, with our staffs on the floor in front of us. I'd sent my staff bearer away, ashamed at the weapon I had forced it to carry. The skin beneath my fur felt raw from the heat coming off the walls outside. I felt as if I'd really been in the Seventh Dimension, summoning Bastet, almost ending the world for all of us.

The feeling was absolutely terrible.

I didn't want my staff anymore, and I could tell by the expression on Seramina's face that she didn't want hers, either. Asinda kept glancing at me with a terrible expression of scorn. I doubted it was because of losing her staff, but rather she probably realised how any marks on our record at the School of the White would delay her next meeting with Lars.

Captain Alliander had her arms folded over her chest, and her gaze was so harsh I could imagine the fire burning behind it. Of course, no fires actually burned in her eyes. Alliander didn't know dark magic like Seramina did.

"I had hoped after Seramina's episode at the Altar of Lore," Alliander said, "that we could trust you three not to summon *Cana Dei*. You, Dragoncat, I had thought would have the most resolve. But it looks like you cannot be trusted after all – none of you can."

Esme stalked in front of Alliander and hissed up at her. Her aggression didn't cause Alliander to take her eyes off me, though. She probably was wondering if I had any more tricks up my sleeve, like a second staff or something.

"You planned this, Alliander," Esme said. "I told you not to hand over the staffs just yet. I told you what would happen, but you wanted this."

I growled. Esme had told me none of this. She was still keeping secrets despite our companionship. Yet it was in a cat's nature to keep secrets; the whole 'trust' ethic had been bestowed upon me by humans.

"It is not your place to make accusations right now, Initiate Esme," Alliander said. "I put these students under your charge, which makes you directly responsible for Dragoncat's actions this night."

"Which is exactly what you wanted, isn't it?" Esme bit back. "Something that you could pin on me."

"Will you be quiet, just for a minute?" Alliander shot back. "I want to hear Dragoncat's version of the story. Why did you do it,

Initiate Ben? You must have known you couldn't possibly get away with it."

Her expression softened slightly, but I knew it was to try and entice some honesty out of me. "I don't know. I was sleeping. I didn't know what I was doing – I *promise*."

"And I can see you still have a long way to go before we teach you how to purify *Cana Dei*. That goes for all three of you." Alliander fixed both Asinda and Seramina with a cursory glance. "I'm sure you can all see now what is at stake."

"There's something else," I said, and Alliander's glare swivelled back to me. "I—" I needed to think how to phrase it. "—in the dream, I was a salmon. I don't expect you to know what one of those is, but it's a big fish. Then, I found myself in the Seventh Dimension, and Arran, and Ammit, and even Apopis were there."

The frown on Alliander's face deepened. "So what did they want?"

I growled, remembering. Could I have called Bastet to that place, even though I wasn't there physically? What would have happened if I had?

I recounted the best possible story I could, not leaving out a single detail. I told my story like the old Ragamuffin back in South Wales used to tell his, to which every single cat in the neighbourhood had swivelled their ears to listen.

I made sure everyone understood the stench of sulphur, the blazing heat, the demon crocodile-lion-hippopotamus with powerful hind legs. Part of me, I guess, wanted to make their skin crawl. I wanted them to understand how real this had felt.

Esme looked concerned. Her deep blue eyes pierced into me, and for a moment I thought she was going to kill me.

"I see," Alliander said, after I had finished. "You clearly remember everything quite vividly, but we still have no way of knowing whether what you saw was actually real."

"It was real," I chimed back. "Arran wanted Bastet. They're trying to kill her."

"Even if it was," Alliander said, "then Arran clearly needs you to complete the ritual, which means the best solution here is to keep you away from *Cana Dei*. Esme, you will continue to train them without their staffs for six months."

"But without an opportunity to practice using their staffs," Esme said, "they'll learn nothing."

"If you're a good enough teacher," Alliander replied, "you'll teach them something. If you do your job well, then when we finally return their staffs, we won't see an incident like this again."

Asinda huffed. She said nothing, but gave Alliander a look that could melt iron.

"Is there a problem, Initiate Asinda?" Captain Alliander said.

"I just want to be out of here, so I can see my boyfriend again. I don't care about my staff and this stupid *Cana Dei*."

Alliander frowned. "Once Driar Lars is in the city and requests your presence, I will be sure to grant leave – accompanied by a guard, of course. Until then, you are to stay confined within these walls."

"I guess I have no choice in the matter," Asinda said. "We're prisoners here."

"If you're immature enough to see it that way," Alliander replied. "Then I guess you are."

12

KEY LOCATION

I slept fitfully that night, again in the basket, feeling too ashamed to go anywhere near the two girls. After everything that had happened at the Altar of Lore, Seramina must have felt responsible for forcing us to live in a school with smelly magical horses and pompous students.

Now I knew exactly how she felt.

The next day's breakfast didn't smell like the previous one, and we weren't allowed to eat until all the other students had left the dining hall. When the White Guard at the door finally let us in, dinner already awaited us in our cloistered area behind the screen.

Seramina and Asinda had courgettes and rice. I could smell so little meat on their plates that I didn't go anywhere near the table. Esme, Max, and I were left the same mushed intestine 'pet food' that we'd been served the previous day. It had been down there a while, left to stew and dry in the heat coming off the wall.

This time, the three of us had no choice but to eat it. But I felt like I deserved it, and I forced it down, knowing that I'd probably throw it back up again later in the day.

Max ate his meal just as eagerly as he had before, but Esme didn't touch a speck of hers. She'd rather starve, it seemed, than lower herself to such a base level.

After we'd had time to eat, Esme once again called us to the centre of the dining hall for our morning lesson. This time, no White Guards oversaw the inside of the room, though one was still posted outside. Now only Esme had her staff, they had no reason to supervise. Alliander, also, had been called out to some mission at Cimlean City's southernmost gate.

Once we had all gathered around Esme, she spoke in a conspiratorially hushed voice. Even so, Asinda looked as if she wanted to doze off. Seramina was looking at Esme with a little more respect, but still her gaze looked glazed and distant. Max kept thumping his tail against the floor. His whole attention was focused on a massive fly that buzzed around, probably in search of Esme's untouched food-bowl.

"Captain Alliander was wrong to confiscate your staffs last night," Esme said.

Asinda's eyes snapped open. "Too right she was."

"But if we're dangerous, then Alliander's actions make a lot of sense," Seramina said, more absently.

"And that is exactly the problem," Esme said. "It seems that we're not the real danger, here. Ben, tell me ... did the dream feel as real as you described?"

"It did," I said. "Ammit was there, and I swear she could have snapped me in two with her jaws if she'd wanted to."

"And Arran wanted you to summon Bastet into the Seventh Dimension. Did he say why?"

"He said he wanted retribution for what Bastet had done to Apopis," I said. "He must be so angry."

"I doubt it," Esme said. She lowered herself to the floor and stretched out her white paws across the warm stone. "*Cana Dei* doesn't do anger."

The Abyssinian turned to Max. He had just caught the fly in his mouth and looked at her proudly as he swallowed.

"Pay attention, Max," Esme barked out in the dog language.

Max stood to attention, "Yes, teacher," he said, panting. "No spells today. Why is everyone so tense?"

"Because Bastet's in danger," Esme whined.

"What? How?" Now Max was barking.

"Max, we really need to know – what did you do with the Key to the Sixth Dimension? What did Bastet ask you to hide?"

Max turned up his nose. "Bastet told me to tell no one. Not a word, even to Corralsa."

Corralsa was Max's jet-black dragon, whom Arran used to ride before he became an evil warlock.

"Max, you have to understand," Esme said. "We respect Bastet's wishes. But she *is* in danger. Arran tried to kill her through Ben's dream."

"But why would he kill Bastet? She hasn't done anything wrong."

Whiskers, what with the volume of Max's barking, I was surprised that guards hadn't come flooding back into the room.

Esme cocked her head. She was on to something. As far as solving mysteries went, Esme was as smart as that man whom I had seen on television sometimes – the one who smoked a pipe and liked to talk incredibly fast. I think he's called Sherlock.

"Bastet has the Key to the Sixth Dimension, doesn't she?" Esme said. "You gave it to her for safekeeping."

Max said nothing, but only whimpered.

"Max, this is important. If you don't tell me the truth, then Bastet could end up dying."

Max still said nothing.

"Oh, for demon's sake, Max," I barked at him. "If you don't say something right now, I'm really going to scratch your nose."

Max could tell he was cornered. His eyes were wide, his pupils dilated. He looked as if the fly he had just swallowed had been an item of the king's finest jewellery.

"Fine," he said after a long pause. "If Bastet is in danger, then I need to tell you the truth."

"So where is Capitut's Key, Max?" Esme said, panting softly.

"Bastet put it in her amulet," Max said. "It's safe there. No one can open it."

Esme repeated what Max had said in the human language for the benefit of Asinda and Seramina.

"Now this changes everything," she said, both in the dog and the human language.

"In what way?" I asked. "What do you mean?"

"I think she's implying," Asinda said, "that we need to get out of here and visit Bastet."

"Yes," Esme said. "Because if Arran can't summon Bastet to the Seventh Dimension, then he's going to try and find another way."

Whiskers – I hadn't thought about that at all. "So we're going to escape the School of the White?"

"I need to find out where your staffs are first," Esme said. "Because I have a feeling you're going to need them."

"But what if one of us loses control?" Seramina asked. "Now both Ben and I have a history. You can't trust us with our staffs, Esme."

Esme looked up at Seramina with narrowed eyes. She didn't need to say anything; her expression told us that she would do whatever it took to stop us before we could summon *Cana Dei*.

Instead, she summoned her staff bearer to place her staff in her mouth, and it glowed brightly along its length. Clearly our second lesson was about to begin.

13

THE PLAN

Esme's doppelgänger was a near-perfect facsimile of the real thing. If you got close enough, you could only just make out the fake scar underneath her eye – present in the glamoured version, but not the real one.

While Seramina, Asinda, Max, and I were sitting on the ground, staring up at an orb of white magic, Esme's glamour strode around the thing, making random comments on it. The real Esme was nowhere to be seen.

Apparently the White Mages, who were stationed in the magical towers spaced out along the walls, knew the type of magic being cast everywhere in the city. But Esme's glamour was a form of white magic, in a school meant for White Mages, and so it would raise no suspicion.

The glamour displayed a magical version of Esme casting another one of those globes of white magic, with the strands of *Cana Dei* dancing in and out of it. This was to be our lesson for the day – or at least any White Mages who dropped in to observe or check on us would see it that way. Max, Seramina, Asinda, and I watched it with faux rapt attention. It was all a part of the act.

Esme meanwhile had cast an invisibility glamour on herself and gone out to do some recon. She needed to find out where Alliander had ordered the staffs to be secured.

"Bengie," a voice came in my head. It had the spiced, deep quality of Salanraja. *"Finally, I've broken through."*

"Salanraja," I replied.

"Why have you been cutting me off?"

"I haven't been doing it intentionally. Cana Dei took hold of me; it was awful. Arran summoned me into the Seventh Dimension in my sleep. He wanted me to summon Bastet – he wanted to kill her."

"You don't need to explain, little one. I'm seeing the events unfold in the images of your mind."

"Good. Now, we're going to escape. We're going to break out of here."

"The other dragons have been telling me. Just be careful, and whatever you do, don't get caught. The punishments that happen to rogue dragon riders are worse than anything you can imagine. King Garmin might order you permanently cut off from your dragon. There's nothing worse than having your bond severed, believe me."

"We won't get caught. We have Esme helping us."

"Esme ... you mean the same cat you've told me many times that you wouldn't trust with a bowl of water, let alone your mackerel?"

"She knows what she's doing, Salanraja."

"I hope so. I really do."

She said no more, having nothing else of value to add. I had a feeling that our dragons would aid us in our escape from the city – once we were outside the walls, they could fly us anywhere. But our staffs were most likely somewhere still inside, and those we would have to get by ourselves.

We must have waited a good solid half hour. I really wasn't sure, because I'd let out a few yawns and then drifted off to sleep.

But cats are light sleepers, and so I awoke as soon as the real Esme entered the room. She appeared just in front of the doorway. Esme's glamour dissipated at exactly the same time, leaving a faint whiff of ozone.

We all leaned in, even Max, keeping silent as we waited for the verdict.

"Well, I was right," Esme said. Her breath smelled of fish. Jealously, I figured that she'd snuck into the kitchens somewhere to grab a bite to eat. "It's not going to be easy to get those staffs."

"Why?" Asinda asked. "Where are they?"

"They're in the most secure place in the city," Esme said.

"Where's that?" I asked. "Oh, let me guess – King Garmin's palace. He probably has a treasure chamber somewhere."

Seramina shook her head slowly. "No, not there. They're inside the Tower of the Grand."

And Esme's knowing look told me that Seramina was right.

14

SNEAKY DOES IT

The sun beat down on us from a cerulean sky. The sunlight filled the courtyard of the School of the White, highlighting each mote of dust that danced over the ground. With all the heat coming down from the sky, the walls didn't need to work very hard to keep the city warm. They let out only a faint glow and they didn't seem to hum, but rather purr.

Unicorns and White Mages milled around the complex. Everywhere we looked they'd clustered together. Tutors and unicorns worked in tandem to cast mesmerising and prismatic displays of light while the students observed. Two male guards stood by the gates, their unicorns on their outer sides. Despite the heat blazing down, their postures remained ramrod straight. Their gazes roved the courtyard in front of them, keeping an eye out for any suspicious activity.

Fortunately, Esme had cast a glamour to render the five of us invisible. So long as we kept close to the barely visible protective bubble that shimmered a couple of metres away from her staff, no one here would see us.

You would have thought sneaking out of the School of the White would have been difficult, although there were moments when I didn't think we'd make it.

At one point, Max almost tumbled into the hoof of a unicorn that was casually crossing the courtyard, a robed guard in tow behind it. I stopped the Sussex spaniel by grabbing onto the scruff of his neck and yanking him back just in time.

With my mouth still full of doggy furballs, just as we were about to sneak right past the guards at the gate, the stare of one them roved downwards. I stopped, frozen in my tracks. He squinted his eyes, and for a moment I thought he'd seen me and was about to raise the alarm.

But he shook his head, took a deep breath, and placed a hand on his unicorn's mane. I let out a breath I hadn't realised I'd been holding, and we slipped through the gate undetected.

"Don't count your chickens or your eggs yet," Esme said, looking back at another set of guards posted outside the complex. "Keep close."

We had departed through the rear gates that led directly into the city. Esme took us down a long street, then we turned a couple of corners leading into a back alley, before she finally dispelled the glamour. Presently, she called upon her staff bearer, which lunged down to pull the staff out of her mouth.

No longer worried about getting caught and being punished as Salanraja had warned, I inhaled a deep breath and took a moment to look around.

The walls inside the city looked no less magnificent than those outside. They still hummed in the same soft tone. Because of the sun, they weren't glowing quite so much. Instead, their inlaid gemstones sparkled in the sunlight, displaying a sense of opulence that told of the wealth of this place. The light also glinted off the cobblestones, which were neatly arrayed along the street, in much the same way.

I perked up my ears to the sound of the crowds in the distance. There was a smoky scent of trout coming from the end of the street that set my tummy rumbling. I guessed breakfast hadn't been nutritious at all.

"Is this your first time in the city, Ben?" Asinda asked, gazing down at me.

I realised that I was the only one here who seemed to be impressed. "It smells so good," I said. "There surely must have been better places to keep us than the School of the White."

That caused Seramina to chuckle dryly. "They wanted to punish us, I guess. They've always said that White Mages are austere. That's why so many of us prefer to become dragon riders."

"But they get to live in a place like this," I said. "I mean, can you just smell that? There's chicken, and trout, and mutton, and milk, and eggs. I always thought cat heaven was up in the sky, but now I know it's in Cimlean City."

At that rather apt moment, a rather chubby looking tabby took the opportunity to leap down off one of the city walls. It turned to regard us for a moment. Soon it seemed to realise we were no threat, and, after a wide and toothy yawn, it skulked off down another alley.

"Always the same old Ben," Asinda said, with a smile. "Always thinking about his stomach first."

"You would be too if you'd had to eat what I had to this morning," I said.

"But it's better than stewed courgettes, right?" Seramina asked.

"Oh yes. Everything's better than stewed courgettes. Not to mention rice – do you know what that stuff does to your stomach?"

Esme let off an amused purr. "Human stomachs are different to cat ones," she said. "They can digest rice."

"I've seen that. But I still don't know how they can like it."

"What are you talking about?" Max asked, growling quietly. "Why don't you ever talk in my language?"

"Maybe you should learn how to speak the human language," I said in the same doggy tone. "Then you wouldn't have this problem."

"I don't have the vocal chords."

"Neither do I," I said.

That caused him to snarl at me as he violently wagged his tail in the air above his rump.

"Let's just stop wasting time," Esme said. She stalked off to the corner of the next alley and peered around it. "Come on."

She vanished around the corner. I considered lingering a little longer, but Salanraja's words echoed through my head: *whatever you do, don't get caught.*

THE TOWER OF THE GRAND

The next half an hour or so of walking felt like absolute agony. For one, I hadn't had any sleep, and with all the delicious scents surrounding me I just wanted to go and steal a fish from somewhere. But also, all my muscles were still sore from the long hike to Cimlean City after Arran had invaded our carriage. It had only been a couple of days ago, after all.

Plus we were walking over cobbles. They might have looked pretty from a distance, but my feet hit them at all kinds of angles, which made them uncomfortable to walk on.

"You are such a moaner," Esme said to me in the cat language, after perhaps my seventh growl.

"I'm just hungry and tired. Can't we at least get some lunch?"

"No," she said. "Be like Max – see how enthusiastic he is."

Indeed, he was bounding along in that goofy manner that dogs have. Every foreign shrubbery, or fountain, or human leg, or anything out of the ordinary became something that he had to rush over to and sniff.

"As a cat, I'm not obliged to say hello to everything I meet," I remarked.

"Well at least you remember that part of your heritage, but still, there's no need for moaning. Besides, we're almost there."

She was right: after just two more street corners, Esme summoned her staff and once again called upon the invisibility glamour. If it hadn't been such a busy street corner, perhaps someone might have been at least slightly alarmed by our sudden act of vanishing into thin air. Instead the crowds seemed far more interested in the fruit sellers across the street.

We wove our way through the throng, and for a moment I worried that Max or I would get lost in the tangle of legs. If we should step out of the invisibility glamour, anyone would be able to see us. We were both peculiar breeds in this realm, and if word had reached the Tower of the Grand that we were missing, the guards would know exactly what features to look out for. Rarely had I seen a cat in this realm with such a marvellous pattern of spots as that which was painted on my own fur.

Esme led us over to a wall made of sandstone bricks, a good couple of feet higher than a tall human. It glowed a little brighter than the other walls in the city, so clearly there was a lot of magic nearby.

"This way, Ben," Esme said.

I saw her leap up onto the wall and cling to the stone with her claws. She climbed up with the most spectacular grace I've ever seen in a cat, and was soon at the top, peering down.

She still had her staff in her mouth, and the glamour cascaded downwards, keeping us invisible from the crowd. I lowered myself into a crouch and then took a leap at the wall too. It was more difficult than any fence I'd climbed back home – hard to get purchase on the slippery stone. But I managed to find my way up after some effort.

Esme touched her nose to mine at the top. "Now I'm seeing more of your feline spirit, Ben. I like that."

"Yeah, and you're that type of she-cat who thinks she can change a tom."

"I'm just reminding you of your true self, Dragoncat. I want to undo all the damage the humans have caused in you."

I ignored her and peered over the edge of the wall. Max was sitting down by Seramina's leg, his tongue lolling as he watched the silver-haired teenager give Asinda a leg up onto the wall. Asinda's fingers grasped onto the top and she pulled herself up like a monkey.

She'd always been an athlete, that one. In Dragonsbond Academy she'd been a champion of all kinds of sports – including the dragon egg-and-spoon. Her dragon, Shadorow, had apparently chosen her because of her deftness. The charcoal beast was one of the most agile dragons around.

Once at the top of the wall, Asinda reached down to scoop up Max, whom Seramina had lifted above her head. The Sussex spaniel scrambled along the wall uneasily. He made an absolute racket scratching at the sandstone blocks as he did so, and he looked like he was going to fall off.

Asinda reached down to pull Seramina up. The younger teenager didn't need to work her arms at all, and so with Asinda's help she could climb with ease.

Together we sat at the top of the wall, the Tower of the Grand rising into the sky high above us. Scattered around the courtyard were white crystals the size of a human fist. Whenever I looked at one long enough it pulsed with light as if it had noticed me. Thin silver lines like rivulets of mercury ran between each crystal, creating a latticework pattern.

"So this is it," I said. "The Tower of the Grand."

As I spoke, the crystals lit up around one of the White Guards. He stopped and turned his head as if he'd heard something. After a moment, he shook his head and his unicorn trotted forwards to continue its patrol.

"Quietly," Esme whispered. "The crystals are very sensitive."

"Sorry," I whispered back.

I turned to Max, who was sitting next to me, half expecting him to start barking. He sat with his tongue lolling low, his head craned up towards the top of the tower. He was panting softly, but the sounds would in no way be audible to the guards below.

"I guess there's no chance of using magic in there," Seramina said quietly.

Esme let out a soft miaow in the affirmative. "Any spell I cast between those crystals will raise the alarm."

"I've also heard," Asinda said, "that they keep over ten White Guards on patrol at any one time."

"True that," Esme said. "It's not going to be easy to sneak in undetected."

"Even as a cat?" I asked.

"It doesn't matter how small you are. Once you step into range of those crystals, the White Guards on patrol will know you are there."

"But they must expect cats. Strays must come this way all the time."

"No," Esme said. "Any local cat that enters here would be immediately shooed away. The local animals learn pretty quickly that there's nothing for them in here that's worth stalking."

"So why exactly are we here, if it's impossible to get in?"

"Because we need to study it. Maybe we can put our heads together and come up with a plan between ourselves."

Other than the crystals, the courtyard was landscaped in the most ornate way I'd ever seen. The lawns looked and smelled as if they had been cut this morning. Pathways wove through them like wild rivers, and apple and cherry trees stood tall, bedecked with fully ripe fruit. My ears latched onto the sound of a horse snorting, and I turned to see a mounted unicorn coming out from behind the tower to my left. Another came from the right, and both unicorns trotted towards each other. The two robed White Guards riding them nodded to each other when they met, and then they continued onwards for another rotation.

"So where are our staffs?" Asinda asked, also peering up at the top of the tower.

The top of the tower bulged outwards, as might a water tower. The highest points we could see were the upper arches of the windows, before the tower folded back in on itself. A light almost as bright as the sun shone out of the windows. It hurt my eyes to look at it.

"Apparently they're in the same room as the King's Crystal," Esme said.

"So – the Crystal Chamber," Seramina said, pointing at the bulge on the tower.

"Where else?" Asinda remarked.

Max turned to me and spoke excitedly, but still quietly. "Are we going up? Are we going up? Looks like a fun climb."

"But there might be wargs up there," I replied.

"Wargs?" he almost barked out that syllable.

"Ben," Esme hissed in the cat language. "Don't encourage him."

Then she spoke softly to Max in the dog language. "There are no wargs. But we can't go up there yet."

"I can't understand anything you're saying," Asinda whispered. "So what's the plan?"

Esme didn't reply immediately, instead watching one of the unicorns pass behind the tower again. The glamour still flowed down from the Abyssinian's staff, protecting us behind its mantle. But if one of us accidently slipped into the courtyard, we'd be spotted immediately.

The unicorns marched in perfect unison, and I could smell that there were other unicorns in the courtyard, performing other patrols.

"Now we've seen it for ourselves," Esme said, "we need a place to give a good think about this. To do that, we need somewhere to lie low."

"I know just the place," Seramina said, and her distant gaze rolled over the bobbing heads in the marketplace beneath us, towards the city slums.

SMELLY HIDEOUT

The midden before us smelled even more like rotten vegetable juice than dark magic does. But unlike dark magic, this actually was due to rotten vegetables, and other disgusting things that belong on middens.

The first whiff of it caused my breakfast to come up the wrong way. The same happened to Max. I looked up at the midden, the back of my mouth stinging from bile.

The heap wasn't the tallest thing in the slums; it wasn't even as tall as some of the two-storey wooden hovels that surrounded us, oil lamps swinging on hooks in their windows. But it was at least taller than the small shack that Seramina led us to, which stood behind a low brick wall and right next to the landfill. The building looked as if it had been constructed of disused planks of wood, of all different shapes and sizes, and huddled together in a ramshackle fashion.

Inside, the shack was currently empty – not a single item of furniture in the large single room. If anyone had once inhabited this place, they clearly had vacated it long ago.

"*This* is your hideout?" Asinda asked Seramina, her fingers pegging her nose.

Humans have an advantage; they can shut themselves off from such stenches with their fingers. Cats don't have that luxury.

"It stinks!" Max barked. "Smelly pile of warg!"

Seramina glared at Asinda, then at Max, who whimpered and went to sulk in the corner of the room. She sat down on the floor and crossed her legs.

"Eventually you'll get used to the smell," Seramina said. "And the White Guard wouldn't even think of looking for us here."

Esme brushed up against Seramina and placed her head on the teenager's lap. It was a bright idea – Seramina's snowdrop perfume would smell much better than the midden. I opted to do the same, purring as Seramina stroked the back of my neck.

"This is good enough," Esme said after a while. "Ben and I won't be here for long in any case."

"Won't we?" I asked. I stretched out my legs, shaking. "Does that mean we're finally going to get some food?"

"First," Esme said, "I want to throw a question to the hivemind. How are we going to sneak into the Tower of the Grand and get the staffs so we can work together to save Bastet? Any thoughts?"

She asked Max the exact same question in the dog language.

He had an idea but, of course, he hadn't quite thought it through.

"I can walk the dimensions, climb the tower in another dimension, then appear inside the tower and take the staffs."

"And how exactly are you going to get the staffs out of the tower?" I asked in dog speak.

That stumped him, and he stopped to think for a while. Though he could travel between the dimensions, the staffs couldn't.

"Just to translate," Esme said in the human language for the benefit of the two teenagers, "Max suggested walking the dimensions to grab the staffs. He won't be able to get the staffs out, but he could get himself in."

"So maybe he could create a diversion," Seramina said. "If he could appear in the right location and then run away, he could confuse an awful lot of the guards."

Asinda shook her head. "We'd still have to deal with the White Mages in the courtyard. There's no way we're getting past all of them – they're not stupid."

"There's also the issue of the barrier around the Crystal Chamber," Esme said.

"The what?" I asked.

Seramina reached out to stroke me under the chin. "I've heard of that," she said. "It can only be dispelled by white magic, isn't that right?"

"Exactly," Esme said. "And the staffs are right behind that barrier. I can dispel it, but you're going to need me to be in the room."

"We've still not worked out how we're going to get through that courtyard," Asinda pointed out.

"Maybe if we flew," I suggested.

"I hope you're not suggesting that we send our dragons in there," Asinda said.

"No, I wasn't. But perhaps you could you turn us all into birds, Esme?"

"No, I can't," she said. "We're not warlocks. Besides, flying over the detection crystals wouldn't stop them from working. We need some way to disable them all at once."

"Or to distract the guards," I said. "Maybe we could ask for some help."

Asinda laughed. "Who would dare do so? Anyone caught aiding us could be sent to prison for life. Not to mention that there's probably a reward out for our capture right now."

"Not humans," I said. "Cats. We need to enlist the help of cats."

"That's actually not a bad idea," Esme said. "But, you know, we're going to have to give the cats something in return."

She looked around as if to give someone else the opportunity to say something. But I didn't give them a chance.

"We'll give them food," I said. "Any cat who helps us can come here to eat. We'll smoke the stench out of this place and give them the finest feast that any cat has ever known."

No one else said a word – because we all knew that I'd come up with the best idea yet.

17

SAUSAGE THIEF

Our first task was to secure some food, and the best place to do that was at the market. It was another half hour walk to get there, and this time we left Asinda and Seramina back at the shack. We thought it wise that they stay undercover, as the White Guard would no doubt be scouring the city for us right now.

This was confirmed when we passed a poster pinned up on the wall of the alleyway. I couldn't read the big word at the bottom of the page, but I could see the perfect black and white oil painting of Seramina and Asinda staring out at us. Their expressions weren't flattering; the artist had made them look like the most dangerous criminals imaginable. No doubt anyone who revealed our location to whomever had put up this poster would gain a fine reward.

As we travelled away from the slums, we saw more and more posters pinned to the walls. The city smelled less of refuse and more of baking bread and boiling soup, and even further in it was redolent of smoked meat and fish.

By the time we reached the market, the sun was already low in a cloudless sky. The crowds had thinned and many of the stalls looked bare. We found a butcher wearing a reedy, wide hat and calling out to the punters.

"Roll up, roll up! Steak, chops, and sausages. We have them all here."

"I think we've found our place," I said to Esme.

"Perfect," she said. "You know, I've never had to steal anything in my life."

"We're not going to do the stealing," I said, glancing at Max, who was sniffing at the corner of the stall.

"Is this it?" he panted in the dog language. "Is this where we get our dinner?"

"We just need to distract the butcher," I said. "You see that roll of mutton sausages there, Max? Just in front of the steaks. That's your goal."

"Got it," he said. "Is it warg meat?"

"What?"

"Warg meat? I've never eaten warg before."

"No one wants to eat warg," I said. "Now don't waste time. Wait until he gets a customer, then you know what to do."

"Ready," Max said.

"Me too," Esme said.

We sat in the corner, waiting, hidden behind two crates of melons. A wiry-looking male customer came up to the stall, pointed at a few steaks and then at the roll of sausages that we wished to steal. He was wearing an incredibly baggy coat with pockets large enough to carry Esme or me in each one.

"Whiskers," I said. "He's going to get those sausages if we don't move now."

"Not on my watch," Esme said.

She crouched back on her hind legs and stared as the butcher reached down and lifted three steaks to place in a paper bag. Then, just as he'd shifted his focus towards the mutton sausages, Esme leaped onto the stall and grabbed a steak in her jaws.

She dragged it off the table and managed to get it quite a way away before the vendor noticed.

"What the – come here, you!"

The vendor bent down to grab at Esme. She couldn't get very far with the big slab of steak, of course. Just before he managed to scoop her up, she reached up with a claw and, hissing, scratched his hand.

"Gracious demons!" he screamed, stumbling after the cat. "I'll show this thing."

It was my cue. I pounced up onto the stall, my focus this time on a pork chop. I clamped down on it with my teeth. The juices of it filled my mouth as I bounded away as fast as I could. Alas, I wasn't very fast at all. The chop was heavier than it looked.

"They're working together!" the vendor screamed, turning. "Come here, you!"

Then I heard someone else say, "Say, that cat's got leopard spots. I wonder if it's the one in the poster ..."

"Could it be the Dragoncat?" someone else called.

"It is! I swear it is!"

"There's a five-thousand-mark reward for its capture. Fifty if we can find its friends."

My heart thumping, I glanced over my shoulder. The butcher loomed over me. His eyes looked greedy, and his meaty hands hovered above me. He lunged.

Whiskers! Forget about the sausages. I dropped the chop, and dashed as quickly as I could through a forest of legs and leather shoes that kicked hard at me. I tumbled from one stall to the other, the sound of barking trailing after me. I hid deep underneath a stall, then shuffled around to assess the cause of the commotion behind me.

The butcher was no longer interested in me. Rather he was pumping his fist with one hand, the other pointing at the wiry man – his previous customer. In the customer's arms was the bundle of sausages. His legs were like windmills, propelling him as fast as possible through the market.

"Thief," the butcher shouted. "He stole my sausages!"

I growled at him from the base of my throat. Not that it would have done anything. Then I saw Max, chasing after the thief, barking.

"Warg!" the dog barked at the top of his lungs. "Greedy, sausage-stealing warg!"

18

CORNERED

Ten minutes later I found Esme in a back alley, hiding behind a locked crate. She looked dishevelled, her fur sticking up all over the place. She had a row of fresh scratches on her right-hand side. I was feeling a little rough around the edges myself. There'd been quite a few large splinters under that stall, and it had been quite a wriggle to get out.

Esme growled as I approached. It wasn't an unfriendly growl, just one of intense pain. I knew it well.

"What happened?" I asked.

"Got into a catfight," Esme replied meekly.

"What? I thought we were meant to be recruiting cats to our cause, not fighting with them."

"I just ..." I walked up to her and started grooming her wound. "That hurts!"

"Just stay still. It will disinfect it. Now tell me what happened."

Esme let out another deep growl that turned into an unpleasant moan. "I just ran into the wrong garden, that's all. There was a marmalade she-cat, and she didn't like me being there at all."

"Couldn't you just have run away?" I asked. "Or used magic?"

"That's what you don't seem to get, Ben. She challenged me, and I had to fight back. I can't use human means to resolve feline conflicts."

"She bit your ear, too," I said, examining it. It was turning purple, and so I was extra gentle as I ran my tongue over it. Esme winced but didn't make a sound.

"After the way I've treated you, you still seem to care for me, Ben. Sometimes I wonder if I'm good enough for you."

"What do you mean?" I took a step back and looked Esme right in the eyes. "You're a daughter of Bastet. Virtually a princess." She blinked at me, slowly. Esme wasn't technically Bastet's daughter – I didn't know who her mother was, in fact. But she'd been raised that way.

"It's all a show," Esme said. "If I behaved like a commoner, the humans would treat me just as they treat you and Max."

"I'm not common. I'm a Bengal, descendant of the great Asian leopard cat, and you know it."

"I know what you are. Still, the people in power don't see you as someone who can assume a position of responsibility. It takes a certain grace to earn their respect like that. Take Alliander, for example. She trusted me with the role of your mentor for a reason."

A butterfly floated by – a brilliantly coloured red admiral, which drew my attention for a moment. My instinct drove me to chase it, but much of what Esme said wasn't making sense.

"Just before, you were accusing me of losing my catness. Now you're saying that you need to be more human?"

"No," Esme replied. "This comes from knowing who I am, and not letting anyone convince me that I need to be anything else. That's why the humans respect me."

She pressed her nose up to mine. She'd not shown me affection like this for a while.

"I still like you, Ben. Even if the positions I have to assume cause me to put you down sometimes."

"I'm just glad you got us all out of the School of the White," I said. "I hate unicorns."

Then I remembered the dream – if I had cast the spell that would have resulted in Arran killing Bastet, I'm not sure Esme might have ever forgiven me.

"You'll stop me doing anything awful, won't you, if it comes to it? I don't want to end up doing what Seramina did."

Esme miaowed a little feline laugh. "I'm not sure you'll ever be that powerful, Ben. But don't worry. I won't let anything happen to you, just like I won't with Bastet. We're kin, after all."

She touched her nose to mine once again, and I chirped to tell her I appreciated her. Then Esme raised her nose and sniffed at the sky. The air was getting humid, and it felt like it would rain soon. She turned her ears towards the end of the street. Smoke drifted towards us from the marketplace.

"Can you hear that?" she asked.

I perked up my ears. Through the bustle of the thoroughfare, there came the sounds of human footsteps and, behind them, a deep growling, snarling sound. As the sounds got closer, they became intelligible in the dog language.

"Greedy warg! Drop the sausages you greedy, inhuman warg."

The reply was in the human language.

"Get off me, you stupid mutt! Why won't you just leave me alone?"

Not long afterwards the wiry man came limping down the street, Max hanging by the lips off his trouser leg. No one seemed to be pursuing him, despite how slowly he was going. Either the butcher was incredibly scared of Max, or he'd decided that counting up his profits for the day and returning to his family was much better for him than chasing down a good kilogram of lost mutton.

"Come on," Esme said, and she rushed down the street towards them. She must have been as hungry as I was, because she'd regained her strength all of a sudden.

I dashed after her and jerked to a stop right in front of the man's foot.

"Put those sausages down this instant," Esme shouted in an incredibly loud human voice that belied her frame.

The man jerked to a stop. "Who said that? I must be hearing things."

He looked around him, his gaze lingering on the doors and windows of some of the buildings. But everything was closed.

"You're not hearing things," Esme said. "Believe me this is very real. Meanwhile, those sausages are stolen property, and you must relinquish them under order of the White Guard."

Max was still growling and tugging at the man's trousers. The man was turning his head around, oblivious. Whiskers, humans could be so stupid sometimes.

"Look below you, buster," Esme said. "You are breaking the law."

The man looked downwards, but then when he saw Esme he let out a reedy laugh.

"You've got to be kidding me. A talking cat?"

"I'm much more than a talking cat," Esme said.

The man's jaw dropped, then his eyes widened as if in recognition. "Please – it's the hunger. You have to understand, I've not eaten all day."

"I don't want to hear any of your excuses," Esme said.

All of a sudden there was a flash of light and Esme's staff-bearer appeared from thin air. Esme's gnarled staff was already aglow by the time the giant hand had deposited it in her mouth. Each of the tiny crystals sent out pulses of magical radiance along its length.

The man blanched. After a moment, he took a shallow breath and then let out a hoarse laugh.

"Say, it's all three of you here. I've read about you on the posters."

"I don't care where you've seen us," I said. "You have our sausages."

The man scratched at the skin underneath his collar. He seemed a little more confident now, despite the fact that an angry dog was clinging to his trousers and accusing him in deep guttural growls of being a warg.

"They've given you names, you know. Dragoncat, Magecat, and the Dimension Walking Dog. It's all got quite a ring to it, don't you think?"

"I said drop the sausages," Esme said with a growl.

"Actually, I've got a better idea. Why don't you three come with me to the closest White Guard constabulary? Then you can have all the sausages you want."

Esme didn't look impressed. "I'm not going to ask you again."

The man puffed out his chest. "Oh yeah? And what are you going to do with your magic inside Cimlean City? It's not as if you can hurt anyone. The walls won't allow it."

Esme chuckled in a human voice. "I might not be able to hurt you with my magic, but my dragon certainly can – with its fire."

She craned her head towards a dark V-shape that had emerged in the sky. From our location it only looked the size of a crow, but it quickly gained distance and soon was above us, hovering over the sausage thief.

Gratis was a black dwarf dragon. He displayed his sharp teeth and opened his mouth to display the fires burning at the back of his throat.

"You wouldn't dare," the man said, tugging at his collar.

"I would," Esme said. "Those sausages are going to need to be cooked sooner or later. It's up to you to decide whether that happens while you're holding them."

A lump of air travelled down the thief's throat as he stared wide-eyed at the dragon.

"Fine," he said, and he dropped the meat on the ground. "Have your stupid sausages. My wife's going to kill me, you know."

Max let go of the man's leg. He continued to bark after the man as he shuffled away along the alley. A warm gust of air billowed down from above. Gratis let out a roar, then swooped upwards, circled once, and flew away.

Presently, I heard the pounding of hooves across the cobblestones, and I caught a whiff of magical horse upon the breeze.

"I guess there was one problem with bringing your dragon here," I said to Esme.

She looked at me as if she'd planned it all along. "Go, Max. Get those sausages back to Seramina and Asinda so they can start cooking dinner. Now!"

Max barked once, grabbed the bundle of sausages, and carried it away with remarkable strength and agility.

The hoofbeats were getting ever closer.

"What are we going to do?" I asked.

Esme summoned her staff bearer and returned her staff to the void. "We're going to go and find the King of Cats."

She leaped up onto an awning and then to the rooftops.

I chased after her, knowing it a better option than being arrested and sent back to the School of the White. Just after I left the alleyway, two unicorns entered with White Guards mounted on their backs.

19

RECRUITMENT

I t was a whole new world above the streets of Cimlean City, and the pigeons seemed to think it was theirs.

Silhouetted by the light of the setting sun, they sat together in twos upon their vantage points. There were pigeons on struts, pigeons on weathervanes, pigeons on the rims of gutters, and all of them looked down upon the scalps of the men and women who still loitered around the market, shopping for last minute bargains before the stalls closed down for the day.

There was the occasional cat on a ledge, too. They were wise and old enough not to pay the pigeons any heed, and certainly not to go chasing after them. When you're a kitten, you come into the world thinking that every bird is there for the hunting. But as you grow older, you learn that birds don't always fly away if you fail to catch them; they also sometimes fight back.

The roofs, it seemed, were just as connected to each other as the landmarks were on the ground. Streets were connected by alleys. The difference here was you didn't pass through the alleys but leapt over them to get where you needed to go.

Esme led the way, leaping from eave to eave and tight-roping over railings. Her paws brushed soundlessly over roof tiles, not slipping once. I followed with nearly as much grace, although in all the time I've known her I've never been able to match Esme's elegance. I wasn't the only tom in the realm who'd sometimes stop to watch her move, in awe.

We eventually reached a tower with a decorative ramp that spiralled around it up to its flat top. Even as a cat it was difficult to ascend, narrowing as it rose. At the end, both Esme and I leaped up onto the roof.

Cimlean City's King of Cats awaited us there. I'd expected him to be a brilliant creature, like a Savannah Cat or a Maine Coon. Instead, he was a small and wiry Cornish Rex – with a distinctive snout and ears almost as big as his head.

He sat with his back to us, grooming himself. In front of him, the Tower of the Grand loomed high, painted red on one side by the waning sun.

As we approached, the Cornish Rex raised his head and looked over his shoulder. As soon as he saw us, he spun around and arched his back.

Displaying a small yet sharp set of teeth, he hissed out, "Stay back!"

Esme and I ground to a halt. Either one of us could take down this rat of a cat singlehandedly, but he was the King of Cats in Cimlean City. That meant if anything happened to him, we'd no doubt have an entire angry clowder on our tail.

Instinctively I also arched my back, and my hackles shot right up. Esme's rump on the other hand was placed firmly on the ground, her forelegs stretched out in front of her.

The King of Cats glared back at me with massive, mustard-coloured eyes. A black patch of fur surrounded one of them.

"Sit down, Dragoncat," Esme said. Then she turned to the king.

"We mean you no harm, Rex—" and I say Rex not just because of his breed, but also that's the best translation from our language of what you might call a cat who has achieved such high status amongst their kin "—we merely come seeking the aid of your colony."

"Aid?" Rex said, and he miaowed a short laugh. "I don't give favours to just any cat who comes asking. Who are you to request such a thing?"

"She is a daughter of Bastet," I said. "And I am the Dragoncat, descendant of the great Asian leopard cat and the mighty George, not to mention a vanquisher of warlocks."

"Shut up, Ben," Esme whispered.

Rex yawned widely. His teeth were so sharp that they could nip through plastic.

"You talk too much, Dragoncat. And Bastet does not exist – she is just a myth."

Esme drew her paws back towards her and lifted herself on all fours. I knew she would be seething underneath her fur, but she didn't show it.

"This is not about who we are, but what we have to offer," Esme said.

Esme turned to her side slightly, and stretched out, displaying her beautiful form.

Rex let out a sound that was halfway between a chirp and a purr. He stepped forward and sniffed at her.

"You certainly smell like a fine specimen."

Seeing him treat her as an object caused me to shoot up and arch my back again, hissing loudly. No one should dare look at my companion that way, not even the King of Cats.

Rex turned to me with a scowl. "Might I remind you of who I am?"

Out of the corner of the eye, I noticed a form slinking onto the rim of the tower. A large ginger Persian tomcat watched me from there, his fur all fluffed up. Persians could be mighty strong, even if they were stupid, so I knew not to get into a fight with one.

"Esme wasn't offering herself as a companion. But we have a feast of mutton sausages – enough to feed your whole colony for a day."

Another cat jumped up onto the rim of the tower. This one was a Manx she-cat with just a stump for a tail. "Did that weird cat mention mutton?"

"That's what I heard," the Persian said, in a very gruff voice for a cat. "Is that a purr I hear? No, it's my tummy rumbling."

Rex laughed and then stepped back to examine me. He seemed, thankfully, to have lost interest in Esme. "Do you know how large my colony is?"

I looked to Esme for help. There was a glint of knowing in her bright blue eyes as she turned back to Rex. "My contacts have told me that you have a good fifty or sixty in your clowder."

"Contacts? Who are you to have contacts? If I find out I have spies in my ranks—" He glared accusingly at the Manx.

"I don't know of any spies," Esme said. "But my own colony has told me of the grand clowder of the glowing city. They say that you're the greatest in the entire land."

"Your colony? And what might that be?"

"Oh, you won't have heard of it," Esme said, and she licked her shoulder a couple of times. "We've travelled far to come here."

Rex sniffed at Esme again. "I thought you smelled peculiar. Well, no matter. But you'd better not be lying."

"We're not lying," I said, looking over my shoulder at the Persian. "We have the biggest roll of mutton sausages that you've ever seen."

The Persian blinked back at me slowly a few times. Promises of food are the best way to make friends in the cat world.

"Good," Rex said. "Because if you're messing us around, there will be consequences, mark my words."

He needed to say no more, for the deal was done. As the sun fell beneath the skyline, he yowled out a discordant song to summon the rest of his colony.

20

IT STINKS!

If anyone was watching the rooftops from the Tower of the Grand, they would have been treated to quite a sight. It's not every night that you can see a colony of cats dancing over rooftops, leaping over alleys, and tight-roping along the most precipitous of ledges, all in pursuit of a common goal. Perhaps they might think that we'd decided to start organising races, or that we'd all teamed up to cull the pigeon population.

Naturally, of course, the pigeons stayed well away from our charge. As soon as any of them spotted our approaching stampede, they lifted into the air and stayed up there, cooing their warnings into the night.

They must have thought that we were out hunting that night. They were probably yakking to each other in pigeon speak – which I could have understood if it wasn't too far away to hear – that the apocalypse was coming. This was the night that the cats were going to bore down upon them, working together to eradicate pigeon-kind. This was the night that they'd learned to behave like wolves.

But our prey had already been caught, and we didn't need to eat pigeon. Of course I was assuming that Max had delivered the mutton sausages safely. I don't know what we would have done if he hadn't.

Esme and I led the way to the slums. As we sprinted, she turned to me and said, "Salanraja says you're blocking her out again."

I didn't need to ask how she knew. Gratis would have spoken to Salanraja, and then communicated it to Esme telepathically.

"My dragon likes to pick her moments," I said, panting the words out like a dog. I'd spent so long on my dragon I'd grown out of shape.

Esme said nothing; there was no need to reply.

I reached out in my mind to my dragon. My heart was hammering, and it was hard to think straight. Still, I needed to know.

"Salanraja ... Salanraja, are you there?"

The voice that emerged in my head was dry yet smooth. *You don't need your dragon. Your bond with it is unimportant in the grander scheme of things.*

Whiskers, *Cana Dei* had returned to my mind. The very sound of it made me slip, and I almost went tumbling off the rooftops. I used my claws to keep my purchase and pull myself back up again.

Steady, Dragoncat. You don't want to show yourself as weak to your kin.

I growled, causing Esme to turn her head towards me and stare for a moment. But another alleyway approached, and we had to focus on the jump. Esme went first, and she sailed over smoothly. But just as I reached the edge I mistimed the jump, and almost ended up falling down into the alley and into a whiff of horse.

My claws latched onto the next ledge, and I looked below to see a White Mage on patrol, his staff raised and glowing brightly. I pulled myself up and returned to running.

After three more rows of rooftops and two more leaps over alleyways, we reached our destination. Alas, it wasn't the mutton I smelled first, but the refuse heap. As we lowered ourselves to the ground, the stench of it made me want to throw up for a second time.

I could only just make out the midden in the darkness. Whiskers, given how it smelled, I was surprised it wasn't also glowing.

Esme and I stopped next to each other. Rex slunk down off the low rooftop behind us and sniffed the air.

"This has to qualify as the worst insult ever," he said.

He turned to me and lifted his right paw, claws extended, hissing.

"Give us a chance," Esme growled back. "Do you want to feed your stomachs or your noses?"

Rex turned to Esme and squinted. "Explain yourself."

"You see that building." Esme turned her head towards the hut. "Just smell the smoke coming from it. Use all of your olfactory senses, for whiskers' sake."

"But why would you choose such a place?" Rex said.

"To mask the scent from other scavengers," Esme said.

I took another sniff, trying to close out the stench of the midden. Underneath it all, if I really focused, I could detect the smokiness of mutton sausages roasting on a fireplace. But I had to concentrate really, really hard.

"There aren't any scavengers in my city," Rex said.

"Really?" Esme said. "Are you telling me there are no stray dogs?"

"Well, they don't come up onto our rooftops. You could have decided to host the feast on a disused terrace."

Esme lifted her head. "What do you think the humans are going to do if they see a fire on the rooftops? This is the best place for a feast, as you shall experience once you decide to step inside."

"And who exactly is cooking the feast?" Rex asked.

"Our allies. Come and see."

Esme glanced back at me, then bounded forwards towards the warmth of the fire. Already the walls were starting to glow around the city, and I knew that it was going to be blazingly hot inside the shack.

"This better not be trickery," Rex told me with a scowl.

Then, he yowled out to call his brethren onwards, then bounded into the shack.

21

NEGOTIATIONS

I'd never heard a room purr so loudly. Seramina and Asinda worked to turn the sausages in the pan they'd placed over a grill on the brazier, while sixty-two cats gazed up at them in expectation. The room was now so filled with flavoursome smoke that I couldn't smell the midden outside at all.

The two teenagers could probably hear the cats saying, "Miaow, miaow, miaow." Like most humans, they no doubt assumed the cats were giving them compliments.

But they actually were saying things like:

"Hurry up, stupid human."

"You're such a slow cook."

And for that hardiest amongst the colony: "Why couldn't you just give us the food raw?"

Esme and I had long left such habits behind us, and so we just sat watching in silence. I didn't doubt, though, that Esme's tummy was rumbling just as much as mine. Meanwhile I was salivating, and all I could think about was the smoky flavour that would soon be rolling over my tongue.

Max, perhaps, was the only creature who actually showed appreciation in a language unintelligible to anyone but me and Esme.

"Smells delicious," he panted. "Can't wait. I'm so glad we're not eating warg after all."

Both teenagers seemed to find it quite entertaining to watch the cats gathered around them, eagerly awaiting food. Somehow the task of cooking a feast had made Asinda seem less irascible and Seramina less dismal. For this night it was as if they were once again good friends.

"I never thought we'd be running a charity for cats," Seramina said.

"Some of them look quite hungry," Asinda said. "Do we get to choose who eats first?"

"I say that one eats last," Seramina chuckled as she pointed at the ginger Persian. "He probably bullied all the other cats to get that fat."

"It's not fat, it's fur," I said. "He's pure muscle underneath it all. But yeah, he probably ate a lot to get there."

"So what about that one?" Seramina asked, pointing to Rex. "He doesn't look well catered for."

Rex turned to Seramina and licked his lips, as if he knew exactly what she was saying.

"Oh, he probably gets the most out of everyone," I said. "The way that his skin stretches over his bones is just his genes."

Seramina bent over to take a sniff at the pan. "Well, I think we're almost there."

Asinda nodded, and she lifted a sausage out of the pan with a fork. I looked up at it hungrily. The sausage hissed, with juices bubbling on the surface of it. Asinda turned it in her hand, examining it from all angles.

The cats closed in, each one trying to miaow louder than the others. Asinda looked down at them teasingly.

"Now who deserves this the most?" she said.

"I reckon Max," Seramina answered, examining the crowd of cats and probably trying to work out the best way through. "He did after all bring us the sausages."

"Don't you dare," I said.

"Absolutely right," Esme said. "Asinda, this is a very delicate piece of diplomacy. Don't drop that sausage on the floor before I've had a chance to work the room."

Asinda chuckled under her breath. She cooed as she turned her head from cat to cat. Some of them, I hate to admit it, were better actors than I.

"Asinda?" Esme said.

Asinda sighed. "Fine."

Still, she continued to turn the sausage around, pouting as she turned her gaze from one cat to another.

"They're all so cute," Seramina said.

Something small knocked into me and brushed right past me. Rex was soon standing right in front of me.

"I get to eat first," he said.

The clowder let out a unanimous moan. But that didn't stop them fanning out to let Rex stand underneath the sausage. He turned to Esme.

"Tell the human that this sausage has my name on it. Otherwise, the deal is off."

Esme stalked forwards and looked the skinny cat right in the eye. "But we haven't made a deal yet, Rex."

"I thought you said you needed help getting into the Tower of the Grand. We distract the guards – then you sneak in with your human friends and that disgusting dog. Easy."

"We still need to discuss terms and conditions," Esme said. "And then we can eat."

There was a pause. Rex clearly didn't like this at all.

"Esme, what's going on down there?" Asinda asked.

"Negotiations," Esme said. "Actually Asinda, put that sausage back in the pan."

"What?"

"Sausage. Pan. Do it. Otherwise, we'll end up losing the deal."

Asinda scowled at Esme, but she did exactly as she asked.

"Now, Rex," Esme said. "Let us discuss terms."

"Eat first, plans later," Rex said.

"No," Esme said with a growl. "My way, or you have to deal with a hungry clowder tonight."

She clearly didn't trust Rex, and rightfully so. If we didn't set the terms now, he and his colony would stuff their faces and then run off into the night.

Rex growled back and raised his back. He opened his mouth and let out a silent hiss. Despite his size, he looked quite scary with that black patch over one eye. But Esme wasn't perturbed. She matched his posture.

For a moment, the two circled each other, their gazes meeting in challenge. Not a single cat, dog, or human in the room intervened. I worried someone would.

Eventually, Rex backed down. He turned his head away from Esme and sat down on the floor.

"Fine," he said. "Just tell me what you want us to do."

"A wise choice," Esme said. "A wise choice indeed."

MILITARY CATS

Not a single speck of mutton remained on the floor. Wherever Seramina or Asinda threw a morsel, a cat immediately moved in to vacuum it up. The fireplace crackled, the cats purred softly, and I could tell everyone in the room just wanted to go to sleep, despite the stench that had started to seep back in from the midden.

Even I felt my eyelids closing. But as soon as they did, a loud yowling sound filled the room.

"Attention, cats!"

This time it wasn't Rex speaking, but the female Manx, who had an incredibly powerful voice.

The cats groaned, and the Manx screamed out again.

"I said, attention!"

"He's awfully loud, isn't he?" Asinda commented to Seramina.

"Not he," I said. "*She*. Can't you tell your she-cats from your toms?"

Asinda shook her head, and Seramina looked at her with a smile.

Meanwhile the Manx continued to bark out orders, whilst the Persian roamed around the room, jostling any cat who was sitting back up onto all fours with his head. Max seemed to be getting all excited by this, and kept running from one spot to another barking.

"Go tell them!" he said. "Go tell them who's boss!"

Rex and Esme sat side by side, casually watching everyone get into formation. I was a little jealous over this, admittedly. The pair seemed to be getting on awfully well. They were like a king and queen together.

It was amazing how fast the Manx and Persian worked to organise the ranks. I'd never seen anything like it. Soon they had all of them formed up in a semicircle, with Asinda and Seramina standing by the wall behind them.

Once he was seemingly satisfied with the formation, Rex stalked forward and addressed the colony. I took the opportunity to join Esme. Her fur, always brilliant and white, had started to look a little untidy, and so I groomed her as I listened.

"We've gone through this a hundred times, but I want to hear it once more," Rex said. "What must we do tonight?"

The cry came, of sixty cats yowling back in unison. "We must stay in the courtyard until sunrise."

"Good," Rex said. "And why are we doing this?"

"So our friends can get into the tower," the colony replied.

Rex turned his head to the side a little. "Speak louder – I can't hear you."

"So our friends can get into the tower!"

"And who needs to get into the tower?"

"The girl, the other girl, the Magecat, and the leopard-spotted cat!"

"And who will help us?"

"The dog will help us with his magic!"

They were referring to the way Max would keep appearing and vanishing as he walked between dimensions, tripping up the detection magic of the crystals in the courtyard. His job was to draw the guards out of the tower, and Esme and I had quizzed him multiple times to ensure that he knew exactly how to do that.

Rex crooned proudly. He turned to Esme, who lifted her head. I started to groom under her neck.

"Have they got it?" Rex asked. "Are you satisfied?"

"They certainly have," Esme said.

"So, we'll meet you at the Tower of the Grand at the appointed time," Rex said. "And remember: if you're late, the deal is off."

"We won't be late. But I hope you also remember the cost of not honouring our agreement."

Suddenly there was a flash of light, and Esme's staff bearer brought her staff hurtling towards her. I barely managed to duck out of the way of it knocking me right on the nose. I turned to see the staff glowing in Esme's mouth and her eyes blazing with warning.

"We will not forget, dear queen," Rex said, lowering his head.

"I hope not," Esme said.

Rex bowed again, and then he stalked out of the room. The Manx headed to the front of the formation and she again yowled out an order.

"March!" she shouted.

The cats followed her out, two by two, with remarkable efficiency. Honestly, I'd never known any colony to work so well together. But then, I'd never encountered a colony so large.

I looked up at Esme, who still had her staff clutched in her mouth.

"What happened to not using human methods to resolve feline conflicts?" I asked.

"They need to know that if they break feline bylaws then we will be allowed to break them too."

I thought about that for a moment, and then decided that this was perfectly fine by me.

✾ 23 ✾

HEIST NIGHT

There were no clouds on the night of our planned heist. Under normal circumstances, the high, bright full moon would have readily announced our arrival. This was why we were cowering under Esme's glamour to keep us invisible.

Together, Max, Esme, Asinda, Seramina, and I sat on the sandstone walls. Seramina and Asinda's legs dangled over the edge on the outside of the courtyard, so they didn't trip the protection crystals. Esme had her staff in her mouth, casting a glamour sphere that glowed slightly on the inside and made us completely invisible from the outside.

High above the tower behind us, the occasional bat flitted over the moon. From beneath us rose the smells of things cooking in the city. Down there was every imaginable type of grilled meats, stews, herbs, and even that weird inedible stuff that humans like to eat, called tofu. The marketplace had really come to life that night. The stalls were now manned with cooks, who were working blazing charcoal grills and massive cast iron pots. The punters ate at the tables from metal plates and bowls.

✻ 97 ✻

I guessed that if we hadn't fed Rex's colony, they would have just come here to eat, begging for morsels. Surprisingly, there wasn't a cat to be seen. Just pigeons, ducking their heads between the tables and pecking at any grain or loose scrap of bread that might have found its way down to the ground.

We waited for a good thirty minutes, everyone silent – even Max. The mounted White Mages behind us couldn't see through Esme's glamour, but they would certainly hear us if we spoke too loudly. There were six guards and six unicorns visibly on patrol in the courtyard. I didn't doubt there were more posted out of sight, however.

We'd positioned ourselves in front of the door to the tower. It was open, and a soft yellow glow was flickering off the inside walls. According to our recon – or in other words the information given to us by Rex – two guards were keeping watch at the door. No one else guarded the tower's interior. The door was large enough for a unicorn to pass through, but they didn't usually allow unicorns inside.

"Are you nervous?" Asinda asked Seramina.

"No," Seramina said, turning her head. "I know exactly why we need to do this."

"Because of Bastet?"

"She healed me that night, at the Altar of Lore," Seramina said. "And she told me that I'd learn to see the light eventually. I didn't hear any of that – I was unconscious – but Ben told me afterwards what had happened."

Asinda nodded. "It's good to know that we have allies out there."

The two teenagers turned their gaze towards the moon. Max went to place his head in Asinda's lap, and she smiled as she tickled his ear.

Soon enough, a small, wiry cat jumped up the wall and came to rest next to Esme. Both Esme and I turned to look at Rex.

"On time, I see," Esme said.

"As promised," Rex said. "My colony always works hard to please our clients."

"Clients?" I asked. "You're not seriously telling me that cats have recruited you before."

"Not cats, unicorns," Rex said, looking down at a passing White Guard. "Geni, our resident Manx, can talk to them. Never asked how she does it and she's never told."

I shuddered. The thing about unicorns is that they don't actually talk to anyone out loud – just through telepathy. So, despite having the gift of all languages, I'd never heard one say anything.

That meant the Manx must have some kind of connection to magic that none of us knew about. It also meant that this colony could easily be in league with the White Guard. They would be able to buy the cats out with a lot more than mutton sausages.

I looked at Esme in alarm, and she squinted her eyes at me, to tell me to keep quiet.

Rex looked from me to Esme and back. He twitched his whiskers.

"Look," he said, "I know the unicorns' riders are looking for you. We could have gone to them and ratted you all out, but we chose to look out for our kin. I just hope you're doing this for a good reason."

I exhaled in relief.

"We are," I said.

I almost added that we were doing this to save Bastet, before remembering that Rex didn't believe in her.

"Glad to hear it," Rex said, and he turned his head up towards the moon.

He yowled into the night. The White Mage looked up towards

him, squinted her eyes and raised her hand to shield them, then shook her head and mumbled something before returning her attention to her patrol. Rex was inside the radius of Esme's glamour spell and so it was unlikely that the White Mage had seen him.

"That's that, then," Rex said. "Let the games begin."

Then, just like that, sixty cats jumped up onto the walls surrounding the Tower of the Grand. They paused for a moment, their forms silhouetted against the moonlight. Then, as one, they leaped down.

The courtyard devolved into chaos ...

24

DISTRACTIONS, DISTRACTIONS

The crystals in the courtyard didn't just glow, they screamed. They made the sort of high-pitched noise that those incredibly fast cars did when their lights flashed blue, back in South Wales. Our old neighbourhood Ragamuffin had warned us all never to cross a road when we saw lights flashing like that. Those cars don't stop for cats, he'd said. They only stop for criminals.

The crystals near where the cats had landed glowed red. Meanwhile, lights ran along the lines of metal that linked the crystals, creating channels that ran out towards where the White Guards were mounted on their unicorns.

The horses whinnied and the White Guards shouted expletives, then they raised their staffs.

The White Mages didn't cast any magic at the cats. They probably thought it wasteful to use such resources for such 'small' creatures. Instead, they swung their staffs in an attempt to get the cats to flee. They were trying to scare the cats away, not to hit them.

The cats did flee, to an extent. But this merely involved

scarpering to the other side of the courtyard and continuing to set off the alarms. True to their word, the cats remained in the quadrangle, not a single one of them leaping back onto the walls. Rex had not let us down.

The whole debacle was a joy to watch, but I knew we couldn't enjoy the show for long. We had work to do.

"Okay, Max," Esme said in the dog language. "It's your turn. Are you ready?"

Max barked, and he leapt off the wall. But he didn't land in the courtyard. Instead, he disappeared into another dimension, using the ability granted him by Capitut's Key.

Moments later, the dog re-emerged right at the door to the tower, again setting off those howling alarms. He dashed inwards and, as we had planned, came out with a White Mage staff that he'd snatched from the rack underneath the table.

"The dog is stealing from us," one of the White Mages said, pointing at him.

"Say, that's the dimension-walker," another said. "Look at his ears."

"Stop him!" shouted a female voice I recognised. But I didn't have time to work out why.

Three of the unicorns turned towards Max, and their horns glowed as their riders summoned magic into their staffs. Max dropped the staff on the floor in front of him and turned towards them, barking. His tongue hung out, and for a moment I thought he was going to let them hit him with their magic.

But just as the beams of white magic came out of the mages' staffs, Max again disappeared into the void. The ground sizzled where the beams had hit it.

"Where did he go?" one of the White Mages asked.

"Behind you, look!"

Max reappeared, the good doggy. He got the unicorns to turn around. Every White Mage in the courtyard had now fixed their attention on him. Two White Mages came out of the door, only one of them carrying a staff.

They went back behind the tower towards where Rex had told us the stables were. I could smell magical horse over in that direction.

"Is this it?" I said to Esme.

"Yes," she said. "Let's go while we have a chance."

She dived down from the wall and I darted after her. The crystals lit up where we landed, and the alarms continued to scream. The glow of the glamour sphere also disappeared. For a moment, we were no longer invisible.

But there was so much commotion that the White Mages didn't notice us. As far as they were concerned, we were just cats causing a commotion. Meanwhile, the guards were trying to catch a dimension-jumping dog.

Asinda wasn't far behind us, leaping off the wall like a chimpanzee that had just had double its ration of bananas, skin and all. She turned to help Seramina down in turn, and they ran after us.

No one was inside – there were just two empty wooden chairs, and a table with a rack for staffs beneath it. The stone staircase had short and wide steps, and this time, I led the way. Asinda and Seramina came up next with Esme at the bottom, still carrying her staff in her mouth as she ran.

A unicorn was waiting for us at the top of the tower. Lieutenant Carmista sat on its back, and she already had her staff drawn. Both her unicorn's horn and her staff were glowing brightly. To Carmista's left was a curved wall of blue light, which I guessed was the barrier that we needed Esme to dispel. I couldn't see anything behind that. In truth, I didn't have time to look.

"Let's try that again, shall we?" Carmista said.

Before Esme even had a chance to cast a counter spell, a large orb of light drifted out from Carmista's staff. It enveloped us and teleported us back to the courtyard where the rest of the White Mages sat waiting on their unicorns.

25

BUSTED

The white light barrier surrounding us and the three mounted White Mages, including Carmista, buzzed angrily into the night. It emanated a fierce heat, and I knew that if any of us went near it, we'd be fried.

The other two White Mages were upholding the barrier by feeding white beams into it from their staffs, which in turn were fed from their unicorns' glowing horns. Esme still had her staff in her mouth, but she couldn't use it. The crystals scattered around the courtyard controlled who could use white magic and who couldn't.

The crystals had now stopped screaming out their alarms. Now that the four of us had been captured, the White Mages had opted to turn to off the whole system. They hadn't managed to catch Max – he'd disappeared into another dimension somewhere.

At this particular moment, I doubted these White Mages cared.

"So," Carmista said. "I only need to go on guard duty for one night, and I end up apprehending you. Captain Alliander had a feeling you would come here."

Asinda strode up to her, and glared up with her piercing cornflower eyes. The static of the barrier pulled on her hair, making it dance like fire.

"Carmista, you have to realise what you're doing here," she said. "Arran is after Bastet, and if we don't do something to help her, he's going to kill her."

"I know exactly what's at stake," Carmista replied. "Believe me, we all do. But what makes you think the four of you can stop Arran?"

Asinda looked to Seramina, who shrugged. We all knew Seramina was much, much more powerful than Arran when she harnessed her powers. But she was also the most volatile – and if history proved to be correct, she was also most likely to be consumed by *Cana Dei*.

Asinda turned back to Carmista. "Are any of you even going to try?"

The lieutenant of the White Guard shook her head. "Captain Alliander made the decision to confiscate your staffs for a reason."

"Answer the question, Carmista," Asinda said. The way she was talking to her made it sound like she'd known her in the past. "Are you going to do anything to help Bastet?"

"You know full well that it isn't my call to make."

"I wasn't referring to you," Asinda said. "I meant, is King Garmin doing anything to help? Does he even know of the threat, in fact?"

Carmista sighed heavily. "Look, I'm just following orders here, Asinda. Besides, don't you think Bastet's able to look after herself? She's incredibly powerful, after all."

"She can't defend against *Cana Dei*," Asinda said.

"And can you?" Carmista asked.

"I—" She looked back at Esme. "I just want Lars back. I just want to get out of Cimlean City so I can see him again. I thought that if King Garmin saw me as a hero, rather than some kind of monster, then ... oh, I don't know." She lowered her head.

Carmista turned her unicorn to one side and reached down to place a hand on Asinda's shoulder. Clearly, Carmista and Asinda knew each other well, but I'd never heard Asinda talk about the White Mage before. Come to think of it, I didn't know Asinda that well myself.

"Just return to the School of the White, put in your good behaviour, and I promise I'll put in a word for you. You'll see Lars again soon."

I couldn't believe what I was hearing – Asinda had given up. I turned to Seramina, wondering if she would display any more resolve. She looked as if she had shrunken in on herself; she looked defeated, as if there was no hope left.

I looked to Esme, trying at least to get some reassurance from her. She glanced at me sadly, then she summoned her staff bearer. The giant hand reached in slowly to take the staff out of her mouth, then disappeared.

You needn't worry, said that bland voice in my head again. The voice of *Cana Dei.*

I closed my eyes, trying to shut it off. But it wouldn't go away.

This is all part of a grander plan. We will be together again soon.

I growled deeply, and Carmista snapped her head around towards me.

"It's nothing," I said. "Just leave me alone. All of you, just leave me alone!"

"When you are back in the School of the White, I will," Carmista said. "Now, this teleportation spell will take a while to cast. It will be best for all of you and for your future if you stay still."

She closed her eyes, and both her unicorn's horn and her own staff begun to glow.

At the same time, rising out of the ground as if from nowhere, came the stench of rotten vegetable juice. I turned to see purple gas billowing up out of the grass. Dark magic. *Cana Dei*, perhaps, or a warlock. Whiskers, if this was Arran, we were doomed.

Another of us, the dry voice said in my head. *Though she resists, she will join our cause eventually. You all will.*

Time slowed, then ground to a halt. The mist coalesced into a loosely human shape. It turned its cloudy head to look down at me, two white eyes glowing with evil intent. The clouds packed together even more, until they eventually revealed the wrinkled face of Lasinta, the oldest of the warlocks. Her clothes materialised around her – a loose, wispy purple cloak that trailed on the ground. She was holding her staff, with its purple crystal on top glowing its native colour.

"Thank you for convincing the White Mages to disable their magical alarm system," she said. "It made it so much easier to get in."

Around her everything was frozen except for me, Esme, and the two teenagers. The unicorns looked taxidermied, and the humans were dolls. Even the white barrier had stopped swirling and pulsing. It was just us and the warlock, and for some reason she had chosen not to freeze us as well.

"You!" Esme said. There came a flash of light from above her to the right. Her staff bearer thrust her staff back into mouth. Now that the warlock had stopped time, I guessed she could use her magic again.

Lasinta looked down at the Abyssinian. A smile stretched across her wrinkled face.

26

AN UNLIKELY ALLY

It was as if time had slowed even more. This time it wasn't because of Lasinta's magic, but rather that my senses had become acutely aware. The smell of ozone mixed with rotten vegetable juice; the bright light of the white magic that imprisoned us, glowing all around us; the static from the barrier pulling on my fur; Esme swinging her staff to the side as if in slow motion, and Lasinta bringing hers downwards.

Two magical beams emerged, one from each staff. White met purple, exploding at the contact point into a prismatic display. Lasinta reached down into her pouch with her free hand and produced a purple crystal. She tossed this over towards Esme, and it landed, sending out another patch of purple smoke.

Esme had no defence. Her pupils suddenly dilated, her body shuddered, and her staff fell to the ground.

"Esme!" Seramina shouted, and she crouched down to examine her.

Asinda, on the other hand, stood frozen on the spot, breathing heavily as she stared at Lasinta. I could see it in her eyes – she was calculating, trying to work out what to do next.

I charged at Lasinta, hissing and spitting. I jumped at her leg, I scratched, and I bit a hole in her trousers. Then I remembered something. The White Guard might have confiscated my staff, but that didn't remove another ability that the crystal had granted me.

I'd been able to transform into a chimera long before I'd found my staff.

I darted backwards, and I willed magic into me. My joints creaked, my muscles popped, and I felt the intense pain of my skin being stretched to accommodate a much more gigantic form.

My tail became a snake, my body stretched into a goat, complete with a second head, and my head ballooned into a third, lion's head as it sprouted the most impressive mane you have ever seen. I made sure Lasinta got the full benefit of my putrid lion's breath as I roared in her face.

"Will you *please* calm down," Lasinta said in her croaky voice. "You may think of me as your enemy, but for once I'm on your side."

"Explain yourself," Asinda said through clenched teeth.

Lasinta clutched her staff in her hand, her knuckles white as she carefully examined me. I flicked my snake tail towards her to let her know that I would attack before she could even try to do the same. Lasinta might be a powerful warlock, but she still didn't have the instincts of a cat.

Lasinta spoke slowly and carefully, punctuating every word.

"I. Want. You. To. Get. Your. Staffs!"

"But why?" Seramina asked, looking up from her spot crouched next to Esme.

"Isn't it obvious?" Lasinta said. "Didn't you see what happened at the Altar of Lore?"

I remembered all of us stuck underneath a massive containment field – a dome of energy stretched high into the sky. The warlocks – in their bird forms – had been trying to get away, as the black gas filled out beneath them.

"*Cana Dei,*" I said. "You were fleeing from it. You didn't want it to consume you."

"Exactly," Lasinta said. "I have my spies, and I know that Arran is moving to attack Bastet as we speak."

She paused, allowing the words to sink in. We were all silent for a moment, thinking of the implications.

"If he gets the Key to the Sixth Dimension ..." Seramina said.

"It's not just about the key," Lasinta said. "Bastet does a lot more in the Fifth Dimension than you probably realise. She regulates the dimensions, keeps them safe. It's her presence that prevents *Cana Dei* from opening portals to other dimensions. Without her, those of us who refuse to succumb to the will of *Cana Dei* are doomed."

But those who don't, Cana Dei said in my head, *can live a life richer than you've ever imagined. Charge her now and take her down while she's unaware.*

I blinked rapidly to try and get the voice out of my head. Even in this place where Lasinta had stopped time, it could still reach me. Lasinta narrowed her eyes and studied me. Could she possibly know?

Not wanting the temptation, I let the energy seep out of my body. The sense of my muscles shrinking down to normal size soothed me. I was soon a regular Bengal once again.

"They can't kill Bastet." Esme stretched her limbs and shook herself as if she'd just emerged from a swim. "She's immortal."

"That's where you're wrong," Lasinta said. "There is one way to kill Bastet: the way to kill an immortal is to send them to a place from where they cannot return."

Seramina shook her head slowly. "There is no such place," she said.

"Actually," Lasinta snapped, "there is. There is an Eighth Dimension. The dimension of nothingness – the void."

"You've got to be kidding me," I said. "Is there any end to these dimensions?"

I'd already found it hard to get my head around the Seven Dimensions, particularly the way the Sixth Dimension linked all the others together. I'd been down so many rabbit holes about the possibilities of that, and then decided that it was better just to accept that I'd never understand.

"This is the last of them," Lasinta said. "Very few know about it, and those who do very rarely talk about it. It cannot be accessed through Capitut's Key, as it is not linked to the other dimensions through the Sixth."

"So how do we get there?" I asked.

Lasinta turned to me. "There is a portal to the void. I believe you can access it in the Fifth Dimension. Bastet knows where it is, though she keeps its location a closely guarded secret. Bastet, they say, is the most powerful magician alive. She has magic that can banish anything from the Fifth Dimension that doesn't belong there. Power beyond us all ..."

"Why are you telling us?" Esme asked. "Wasn't it you who tried to steal the key to the Fifth Dimension in the first place?"

Lasinta shook her head, and her gaze grew distant. "Do you not understand? I could hold so much power with the key. But if the cost is the destruction of us all, I do not want it. Though we are enemies, we currently share a common goal."

"What are you suggesting we do?" Asinda asked.

"Destroy the key," Lasinta said. "Send it to the Eighth Dimension and stop this threat once and for all."

"I really don't think we can trust you," Seramina said.

Really, I think that went without saying; none of us could trust Lasinta. These warlocks had betrayed us too many times.

Lasinta cackled. "Really, I don't think you *should* trust me. But what's the alternative for you?"

"Surely you could stop Arran yourselves," Esme said. "Aren't you warlocks going to get involved, if your lives are in danger?"

"No," Lasinta said. "No, we are not. We'd much rather you all risked your lives for it."

"And why would we do that?" I asked.

"Because you're all good, and we're evil," Lasinta said with a wry chuckle. "So you get to go first."

27

INSIDE THE TOWER

Lasinta disabled the barrier of White Magic that surrounded us first. She brought it down with an incredibly smelly cloud of dark magic. Because time remained still, the barrier didn't sputter or fade or anything like that. It was just there one minute and gone the next.

Everything in the courtyard was frozen: cats, unicorns, White Mages, wisps of grass that should at least be blowing lightly in the breeze.

I could still see the bats flitting over the moon and hear the bustle of the night market. Time, it seemed, had only ceased to exist in the courtyard. It made me wonder what would happen to the time that everyone inside the courtyard had lost.

With me, you will no longer be troubled by paradox, Cana Dei said in my mind.

Whiskers, I really wished it would shut up. It was honestly more annoying than Salanraja could be. Sometimes I looked back fondly on the time when the only conversation I ever heard in my head was with myself.

Lasinta kept her staff held out, the crystal on it glowing while it held the spell, as she led us up the tower. When I'd rushed up before, I hadn't remembered there being so many stairs. But then, we had been in a hurry. Now it seemed we had an infinite pocket of time, so long as we stayed within the confines of Lasinta's spell.

I was out of breath when we reached the top – so much that I was wheezing slightly. Seramina also seemed to want to collapse to the floor. But both Esme and Asinda looked like they'd just stepped out of their front door for a morning stroll. Strangely, Lasinta didn't seem fatigued by the climb either. I guessed it was all a part of her magic.

Lasinta turned towards the barrier of blue light that surrounded us. It cast a cool ambience over the outer wall of the tower, and the night behind the tall windows contrasted starkly against it.

Unlike the latent white magic in the walls of the city, the barrier didn't let off any heat. Instead it seemed to suck it away, like a wall of ice. If I stared at it for more than a moment, I could make out patterns of light dancing upon its surface.

Time, it seemed, had returned to normal. But I guessed everything was still frozen outside. Otherwise we'd have had a whole stampede of unicorns rushing up the stairs after us.

"I hear you have a new nickname," Lasinta said, looking down at Esme. "So do the honours, Magecat."

"And why do you need to be up here with us?" Esme asked with a growl.

She held her staff firmly between her lips. I'd always wondered how she could talk so eloquently like that, and I'd always assumed it was through magic.

"Because I'm casting the spell that keeps those unicorns away," Lasinta said. "Now stop wasting *time* or I might accidentally run out of magic."

"Fine," Esme said.

She closed her eyes. Her eyelids glowed white as she summoned the magic into her staff. Her whole body shook as she did so. Her staff shone so brightly that it looked as if it was going to explode.

At the same time, the chilly wall that ran to the left of us also lit up. First, white sparkles flickered over its smooth blue surface. Then the whole thing shone white, letting out a high-pitched whine that caused me to flatten my ears against my head.

It was so bright that I had to close my eyes, and I saw spots before them.

A warmth washed over me, and for a moment I was in a field of long grass, dandelion puffs rising high into the sky all around me. Seeds floated away, underneath a golden sun. The world hummed with flies, and bees, and dragonflies. I saw a bright crystal at the centre of the field. It hovered in the air and spun around on its axis – my crystal.

It spoke to me in its smooth lilting accent that I'd come to know so well. The voice was both in my head, and also filling the space within my ears.

"There will be a cost to this, Dragoncat. There always is when you sacrifice trust to gain favours from the wicked. But there are times when you have no choice."

In the dream I blinked, but in the real world, my eyes stayed shut. The crystal was talking about Lasinta. Whiskers, I should have known she would have an ulterior motive.

I opened my eyes to see the room behind where the barrier had been. The most gigantic crystal I had ever seen loomed over the centre of the room, hovering above a pedestal. Its facets displayed visions of the world like you might see when watching the television in fast-forward mode – the possible futures of people I'd never seen before flashed by one after another. Lasinta was already in front of the King's Crystal, leaning hungrily towards it, her staff held out before her. Beneath the crystal, our three staffs lay neatly arranged, one in front of the other on the floor.

"This is it," Lasinta said. "Finally, I have been granted the opportunity."

"What are you up to, Lasinta?" Esme asked. She had her staff turned towards her, ready to strike.

"It will only take a moment," Lasinta said, and she touched the crystal on her staff to the much larger crystal.

All of sudden there came a boom as loud as thunder, and the contact point between the two crystals flared with brilliance. The light filled the room. It was followed by a much quieter wheezing sound.

The light faded ...

Lasinta had gone.

All that remained was a trail of purple gas leading over to one of the tall tower windows. Through it, I could make out the silhouette of a broad-winged condor, flying towards the moon.

28

SNACK TIME

Esme and I sat side by side on a bench at a table beneath the outer wall of the Tower of the Grand. From inside the court-yard came the calls of White Guards shouting orders; I could hear Carmista's voice in there somewhere, but not what she was saying.

The air smelled deliciously of the remnants of battered white-bait that lay on the bench between us. Admittedly they were now just piles of bones. They'd been sourced from a bowl on the table that Seramina had procured.

Honestly, after our feast of mutton I'd thought I'd never eat again. But the commotion in the tower had made me hungry, so I guess it was only natural.

Every so often White Guards trotted past us, stopping to ask the punters if they'd seen anything in the marketplace. They hadn't. Time had been slowed just long enough for us to escape from the courtyard, and as soon as we were away from its crystals we could cast magic again.

Esme had cast the glamour to keep us invisible as we wove our way to the table, whilst Seramina had cast a glamour on herself to make her look like a middle-aged, brown-haired lady with a hairless mole on her right cheek. She had used this visage to purchase the whitebait from the market with a few spare coins she'd had in her pocket.

Now Seramina held her staff in her right hand – the butt of it placed firmly on the cobblestones – while she munched on the whitebait with her left. She wasn't just casting a glamour over all of us, but also the table and the food as well. If anyone even came close to our table, risking bumping into it and revealing our location, Seramina pointed her staff at their foreheads and cast a mind magic spell that convinced them to turn away.

This happened a few times, but not very often. The night was now getting old, the crowds in the night market had thinned, and most of the city was asleep.

Seramina had been mighty hungry; I could tell that by the less-than-neatly-picked pile of fish bones she had in front of her. Asinda, on the other hand, had hardly eaten a thing. She gazed up dreamily at the Tower of the Grand. If she was arrested now she'd be in a load of trouble, and might never see Lars again. But if what Lasinta had told us was true, then we didn't have a choice. The onus of responsibility to protect Bastet fell on us.

Seramina reached out and took Asinda's hand. Asinda turned to the silver-haired teenager and displayed a concerned frown.

"I'm sorry," Seramina said.

"For what?" Asinda asked.

"We keep dragging you into things that you don't want to be a part of," Seramina said. "If I hadn't summoned *Cana Dei* at the Altar of Lore, then you'd be with Lars right now."

"Yeah, and none of that would have stopped Arran going after Capitut's Key," Asinda said. "We do what we have to do to be heroes – we have to make sacrifices, right? Even if it means we might lose our loved ones."

Seramina shrugged, but said nothing. I gazed at Asinda, wondering if she'd also spoken to her crystal when Esme had been dispelling the glamour.

"I wonder what happened to Max," Seramina said after a moment.

"Oh, I'm sure he'll join us when he's ready," Asinda said. "It's hard to lose a dog like that."

"That's true," Seramina said.

"I just wish I could say the same for Lars," Asinda said, and she closed her eyes and inhaled deeply.

I leaped up onto the table, happy that I was allowed to do so in this world. I slinked off it onto Asinda's lap, and pushed my head into her belly, purring. Asinda let out a deep sigh, then reached down to stroke my back. I turned over and let her rub my belly. She didn't need words right now; she just needed the feeling of warmth against her. We all need a little comfort sometimes.

Esme was already up on the table, looking down at me jealously. She miaowed at Asinda. She might have been a high and mighty princess, but at heart she was still a cat.

"Come here, Esme," Seramina said. "Leave Asinda to Ben, and come keep me company. I am, after all, the one with the fish."

Esme miaowed again, sounding quite content with that offer. I raised my head – or you might say I lowered it given I was upside down, and dreamily watched Esme slink off the table onto the bench next to Seramina. She rubbed her head against Seramina's hand, then she lay down on the bench, laying down her head next to her thigh.

For a good ten minutes or so, my throat and Esme's were in competition for which could produce the loudest purr. I was the happiest cat in the world. I'd had two excellent meals that day, I'd retrieved my staff, and now we had time to finally lie down and relax.

"*Bengie, there you are,*" a familiar voice said in my head.

"*Salanraja,*" I said. "*I … I'm sorry, this* Cana Dei *thing, it keeps wanting to block me off, and I don't know why.*"

"*I know,*" Salanraja said. "*I'm trying to work it out with the other dragons. But it's not just you.*"

"*What do you mean?*"

"*The others,*" Salanraja said. "*They've been keeping quiet about it, but you're the only one any of us can reach right now. We're all a bit concerned.*"

I looked up at Asinda in alarm. For a moment I thought I saw the spark of a fire behind her eyes. But surely I had to be imagining it. When I looked for it again, I couldn't find it.

Then I looked over to Esme, who was batting with her paw at a piece of whitebait that Seramina was holding over her head.

"*What about Esme?*" I asked Salanraja. "*She's got the white magic to protect her.*"

Salanraja said nothing.

"*Salanraja?*"

Oh, do be quiet, said the voice of *Cana Dei* in my head. *You had your moment to chat with your dragon. But such times can't last forever.*

Time seemed to stop once again. This time, though, it wasn't due to magic but to heightened awareness. My body froze, and it occurred to me that my friends might not be my allies after all.

Seeming to recognise my concern, Asinda once again reached down to tickle my belly. But her hand felt cold to me now, and from somewhere I imagined I could smell rotten vegetable juice. I growled at her, pushed her hand away, and leaped back over to the other bench so I could have some time to myself.

29

THE TALKING UNICORN

The east side of the city was the merchants' quarter, and it was the most opulent part of Cimlean City. That meant more shining gems in the walls, higher towers with golden domes, bigger cobblestones, and a rich scent of jasmine and pomegranate around every street corner.

We wove our way through all of it, towards the North Gate. After a short discussion, we'd decided that it was the best place to escape the city. The gate wasn't usually as well guarded as the others. This was because it opened out onto a five-hundred-foot drop onto the plains below, with only a narrow merchant path between city and crag.

Out of all of us, Seramina had the strongest mind magic, and that included glamours. So she led the way, holding her staff in front of her – although we couldn't see her staff. Her goal wasn't to make us invisible now. Instead, her magic had transformed her and Asinda into much older-looking White Mages, both of them male. They both had the same long red and white hair. They also had hard edges to their faces, and in all honesty they both looked pretty mean.

Esme and I now looked like unicorns, much to my chagrin. Esme even smelled like horse, and I made sure to remind her of this at every corner. At first she ignored me. Then she reminded me that I also smelled of horse.

"Yeah, but it's a magical horse," I said.

"Which makes it worse, right?" Esme asked.

"Definitely," I said. "No creature smells worse than a magical horse."

We reached our destination absolutely exhausted. I'd expected a tall wooden gate, like all the others I'd seen in this city – indeed, this gate was certainly tall, but it wasn't made of wood. Instead it was constructed of some kind of shiny brushed steel, with golden swirls and curlicues across its surface. Really, I'd never seen anything so pointless in all my life.

I mean, we cats also have art, but we don't shape it into place using hammers and anvils. Rather, we spray it out of our behinds.

A large plaza lay at the foot of the gate, sporting two cherry trees with fruit ripe for humans to eat, while cats snoozed lazily in the branches on either side of it.

Two guards waited for us at the gate. As Esme had promised, they were regular guards wearing normal steel armour. Each carried a halberd with a scarily sharp-looking tip. One was a man with a bald pate, the other a woman with a brown eyepatch over her left eye.

"Halt!" the female guard said. "Papers, please."

Seramina looked at Asinda.

"Papers?" Asinda said in a remarkably realistic gruff voice. "We're White Mages – we don't need to show our credentials to guards. If anything, you should be showing your papers to us."

"Orders of the king," the female guard said. "No one can pass through without proper documentation."

"But King Garmin has ordered us to patrol the Scalio Crag,"

Asinda said. "He's organising a hunt tomorrow. In the same location as a recent warg sighting, I might add."

The female guard turned to her comrade. The male guard raised his eyebrow, displaying several deep wrinkles on his forehead.

"Heard nuthin' about wargs out—"

Seramina interrupted the guard, her voice sharp. "What's your name, soldier?"

The guard stood to attention. "Con, sir. Private Con."

"Tell me, Con, do you really want to be responsible for a king with a maimed leg?"

Con scratched his cheek. "Well I—"

This was so much fun. I really couldn't resist joining in.

"Warg attacks shouldn't be taken lightly, you know," I said. "Imagine what it would be like standing face to face with a warg."

The female guard's eyes went wide. "Say, did your unicorn just talk?"

The male White Mage that was Asinda turned around and glared daggers at me. "You must be hearing things, private."

"I heard it too," Private Con said. "Just wait here a moment."

He turned slowly, and then raised his hand to a string that dangled down a post from a large bell.

"Oh, no you don't," Seramina said, and I saw her staff appear in her hand.

All I needed to do was blink, and Seramina was the same silver-haired teenager again, amber flame burning at the back of her eyes. We'd all lost our glamours, in fact, and Esme no longer smelled of horse.

A beam of purple magic came out of Seramina's staff. It hit Con right in his hip. He froze in place, his hand stretched out towards the alarm rope.

"What the—"

The female guard didn't manage to complete her sentence

before Seramina sent another beam into her chest. The magic froze her too, an expression of confusion twisting the visible part of her face underneath the patch into a tightly wound knot.

"What in the name of the king is going on here!" a male voice boomed out.

I spun around to see the White Mage, Lieutenant Larmend, approaching on his unicorn from the other end the square. The sun glinted off his bald scalp. Two mounted White Mages trotted on either side of and slightly behind him.

All three of them had their staffs drawn, ready to attack.

30

OLD FRIENDS

The wind whistled through the cherry trees in the square and buffeted around them, kicking up dry fallen leaves in swirls. The air was charged with static as the staffs belonging to the three White Guards on their unicorns glowed. Behind us, the great metal gate that was meant to be our escape from the city creaked in warning.

The city guards frozen by Seramina's magic stood next to the gate, making our crimes obvious. We hadn't just tried to escape – we'd also assaulted two guards.

Seramina had her staff drawn, and the fires burned deeply at the back of her eyes. I caught the whiff of rotten vegetable juice upon the breeze as the crystal on her staff begun to glow purple.

Asinda placed her hand on Seramina's arm and pulled it downwards.

"Seramina, you really don't want to do this," she said.

The silver-haired teenager turned to Asinda. For a moment, I thought nothing had registered. But then, Seramina took a deep breath and lowered her staff.

"Put your staffs on the floor," Larmend said, "because I don't want to have to take you by force."

Both Asinda and Seramina lowered their staffs in unison and placed them gently on the ground. Seramina had assumed her same dejected posture. Asinda was breathing deeply, with deliberate breaths, as if trying to calm herself down. Clearly they'd both given up, and in all honesty I had as well. We didn't have a way out of this. We'd been foolish to think that we could escape the White Guard in the first place.

Summon your staff now, the voice of *Cana Dei* said in my head. *I can show you how powerful you are.*

But I'd had enough of that voice. I'd had enough of everything; I just wanted to curl up in a warm corner and go to sleep.

"That goes for the two of you," Larmend said, pointing at me and Esme in turn. "I want to see your staffs on the ground."

There's your opportunity. Use me. Claim my power and eliminate your adversaries. The solution is well within your grasp.

For a moment I was tempted, but that image of Seramina fainting at the Altar of Lore after *Cana Dei* had almost destroyed her entered my head. That memory protected me. Perhaps it even saved us all.

Salmon. Just think of the salmon you can be eating right now. All the smoked salmon you could ever want.

It was a desperate plea, because *Cana Dei* knew it had lost this battle. It had failed to gain dominion over my thoughts. Despite the grave situation, at least I had that victory.

Esme took the lead by summoning her staff bearer. The gigantic hand lowered itself to the ground and placed Esme's staff neatly on the cobbles in front of her. I willed my hand to do the same thing, and it did so with grace and flourish. If we were going to go down, we would do so in style.

"Have we lost?" I whispered to Esme in the cat language.

"Just wait … I've been talking to Gratis about our plan."

"What? You can reach him?"

"Of course. Why wouldn't I be able to?" Esme twitched her whiskers.

"Will you two shut up?" Larmend said. "I don't want to freeze you like you did with our guards here."

I growled at him and decided it better to groom myself than to attempt a conversation with my companion. Larmend closed his eyes and his eyelids turned white as his staff glowed brightly. If he were casting a teleportation spell, I knew I would have a little time to give myself a good clean.

The air suddenly shimmered behind the unicorn.

A squat, floppy-eared dog emerged out of nowhere, coloured liver-brown. It barked up at the unicorns. The one on the left whinnied and tossed its head.

"I'm here!" Max shouted. "I came to save you! I brought help!"

I immediately jumped back onto all fours, shouting at him in the dog language.

"Who?" I asked.

"Up here," called a voice, and I turned my head up to see the lanky form of my old friend Initiate Rine standing on the parapet. He was a dragon rider, just like us. Cocky but loyal.

He held his staff, the blue crystal upon it shining. Rine cast a blue beam out of it which erupted when it hit the ground into a tall wall of ice that separated us from the White Mages.

Another woman emerged on the opposite wall, with a small and triangular face. It was Ange, and she also had her staff in her hand, this time shining green.

"Through the gate," she shouted.

"But it's closed," Asinda shouted back.

"Not for long." Ange directed a green beam of light from her staff at one of the cherry trees.

A massive root tore out of the cobblestones beneath the tree. It snaked quickly towards the gate, rending stone and earth as it went. Once there, it split into two branches, which lurched out of the ground and pounded against the steel. The gates slammed open.

The four of us didn't waste a moment charging towards the opening. On the other side was the cliff, leading down into a drop filled with white mist. A chute of ice led down from the wall on one side, and on the other was a wide branch, sturdy and straight like that of a pine tree.

I heard a cry of, "Geronimoooo!"

Rine came sliding down the ice chute. Ange walked more casually down the branch. Max also appeared on our side of the gate, out of nowhere. Whiskers knows from which dimension he had come.

On the other side, the White Mages had already found their way around Rine's ice wall, and their unicorns were galloping towards the gate.

Ange was quick to cast another beam of light into the roots at the base of the gate. Vines and branches spread out of them, forming a solid wall like the densest of rhododendron bushes.

"We'd better run for it," she said. "Our dragons are waiting just a little to the south."

She was right on that point. In single file, we sprinted along the narrow path.

Larmend's angry voice trailed behind us.

"You won't get far," he called. "You'll see."

Shortly afterwards, heat blazed out from the wall beside us, flaring bright white. A high-pitched keening sounded out from the towers of the city, and the cry spread out from tower to tower, as if a hound had started barking to awaken a whole neighbourhood of other dogs.

"Well that's done it," Asinda said. "They've set off the alarm."

They certainly had, and it was hurting my ears so much. But I couldn't let the pain stop me, not if I didn't want to get caught ...

31

RUN FOR IT!

We'd run so much in the last few days that one might have thought we were training for a race. Races are human inventions and rather stupid in my opinion, which is why cats don't tend to partake in them. But the path we sprinted along felt just like one of those racetracks I'd seen on the television.

With one exception – human racetracks are safe. Our track had a precipitous drop on our left, a blazing hot wall on our right, and a sandstone path that kicked up so much dust it made me want to sneeze.

We ran into the night so fast that none of the humans had any chance to speak, apart from Asinda. So it was she who answered my complaints.

"Can't we just cast magic?" I asked.

"I don't think so. Not while there's an alarm," Asinda said.

"How so?"

"Because the towers are feeding the wall extra power."

"You what?"

"More power, greater radius of protection. Look, just focus, Ben."

"Fine ..."

I carried on running so fast that my legs burned. The wind buffeted at us from the cliff as if it wanted to knock us into the blazing wall.

"Where's Palimali?" I asked. Palimali was Ange's cheetah.

"I don't know!" Asinda shouted back.

"Ange?"

Ange's voice came back between gasps. "With ... the ... dragons."

I heard some cries from above and caught the glint of the sun off chainmail. There came a whistling sound, and my instinct told me to swerve to the left. Something tickled my tail, and I turned around to see an arrow buried into the ground just getting ready to topple over.

"Archers!" Asinda cried. "Get closer to the wall."

"But it's blazing hot," I said.

"Better that than an arrow in your behind, believe me."

I didn't have enough breath in my lungs to ask whether or not she was speaking from experience.

We swerved to the right. One of the archers cried out from the walls. My ears homed onto the sound of a score of bowstrings tightening. They sounded like harps whispering in the wind.

"Loose!"

I didn't even think about it. My body lurched towards the wall and I groaned against the pain of the heat.

Whumpf.

A row of arrows hit the ground to our left, plumes of dust rising up all around them. Then I felt a hot stinging pain to my right. I'd ventured too far away from the arrows that I was almost touching the wall. I swerved back on course.

Max was barking. "Wargs! Wargs! Aggressive shooting wargs!"

I don't know why he didn't just disappear into another dimension.

We approached another guard tower up ahead. I saw more archers up on the wall. I couldn't see the bows and arrows, but I saw how they had one arm nocked slightly behind the other.

Whiskers, we were going to die.

Another cry came from up ahead. The archers ahead pulled back their rear arms.

"Nock!" came the cry from the wall.

"We can't make it," I shouted.

"Just keep running," Asinda said.

"Draw!"

I wasn't focusing on my burning muscles or the ground ahead of me. My heart pounding in my chest, I was waiting for that imminent cry of, "Loose!"

Instead, I saw a flash of golden light. Or not one, but many flashes, twinkling on the coats of armour ahead like sunlight off the water.

Next thing I heard was a *cluck, cluck, click-cluck.*

The shiny armour of the archers had turned into white feathers. I saw the orange beaks and the red crests on their heads, and I knew that the guards had suddenly become chickens.

But how?

I continued to run. My legs were burning and my head was spinning. There was no time to think; I just needed to accept things as they came.

A golden wisp darted awfully close to me, then whirled in front of my vision like one of those evil midges. It landed on my nose. I went cross-eyed, only to see a man standing there.

I knew him.

That pretty face. The oiled black hair. He was the last person I wanted to see that moment. Or, should I say, the last fairy ...

"You're welcome, Dragoncat," Ta'lon said in the fairy language. "Ta'ra sends her regards."

I growled. Prince Ta'lon was the fairy who'd stolen Ta'ra off me. Why couldn't we have been saved by someone else?

"I don't like you," I said in Ta'lon's language.

"Well, that's too bad. Because Ta'ra does," Ta'lon said. He flew off, chuckling to himself. Fortunately, because he was so tiny, I didn't hear him laugh for very long.

We passed the guard tower with the clucking chickens on top of it. They can't have been very loyal guards, because truth be told there were probably enough of them to fly down and overpower us.

I could see our dragons ahead of us now. Salanraja stood in advance of the others, her head craned up as she watched us approach. I still couldn't hear her inside my head. A massive white dragon was amongst the throng: Olan, Aleam's dragon. Which meant our old mentor must be part of the plan to rescue us.

"Lars," Asinda cried out. "Camillan is there, which means Lars is too!"

But we weren't there yet. Something pounded the ground behind us, shaking the earth. A large stone tumbled off the cliff edge nearby and plummeted down to the floor. I looked over my shoulder to see five unicorns charging towards us. White Mages sat bareback upon them with their staffs drawn, ready to mow us down.

"Just a little further," Asinda shouted.

I hoped so, because my legs were now cramping so much that I just wanted to give myself up.

We had reached the end of the wall. To our right, I heard more hoofs pounding. Another team of unicorns was galloping in from that direction.

The dragons were off to the left now, and we sprinted that way. The old man, Aleam, stood in front of the dragons, his brown cloak billowing. Lars stood next to him, his expression urgent.

I couldn't see Asinda's face, but I could only imagine the hope in her eyes.

But the unicorns behind us were almost upon us. The unicorns to our right were also closing in fast.

"Stop in the name of the law," the White Guard at the front shouted. It was Alliander.

We were so close. The dragons had turned their backs towards us. Our legs churned through the long grass. We only needed to scramble up their tails and they could carry us off towards freedom.

Behind us there came a flash of light. A beam went right over our heads in an arc and landed behind Aleam and in front of the dragons. A wall of white light, spread out in an arc, making it impossible for us to reach our mounts.

"I said stop in the name of the law," Alliander shouted again.

There were a lot of unicorns. I could hear the full weight of their hooves now. So by the time we had reached Aleam I knew that we had lost.

There was no escaping now.

32

A MIGHTY KINGDOM

The two troops of White Guards who had been involved in the chase numbered around a dozen apiece.

Lieutenant Larmend headed the troop that had followed us from the east gate, while Captain Alliander was in charge of the other. Both she and Larmend had their White Mages and unicorns focused on reinforcing the wall of magic that separated us from our dragons. The light looked so bright streaking in arcs over our heads. There was no way any of us was going anywhere.

The White Mages didn't look happy. Honestly, I couldn't blame them – we'd raised an alarm in the middle of the night, waking the whole city. They'd probably be talking about this occasion for years.

Now the alarm had stopped keening out from the towers, so at least the citizens could sleep. The walls had stopped blazing with so much intensity, but a warm breeze still wafted out from the city.

"*Bengie,*" Salanraja said in my head. "*You've opened your mind again.*"

"*I kept it open all along,*" I said. "*And just because we've not spoken for a while, doesn't mean you have permission to start calling me that."*

I'd hated being called Bengie by my master and mistress' son back in South Wales, and I hated being called it by my dragon even more.

"Fine, Ben. If you insist. Gracious demons, I've finally reached you. Aleam and Olan were right all along."

"Right about what?"

"Let's just say things are worse than you think."

My whiskers twitched. *"What? That's not telling me anything."*

"Just stay focused. Aleam will explain soon, but he might need a little evidence from the five of you. You need to make sure you hear every word."

The seven of us – two cats, four teenagers, and a dog, stood huddled behind Aleam and Lars. Asinda, naturally, had moved awfully close to Lars. But she hadn't made contact with him yet. Both Aleam and Lars were now Driars, or in other words dragon riders in service of the king. All five of us were still Initiates – in other words just students. We needed to leave this upcoming exchange to the authorities.

Rine and Ange stood next to each other, with the desert cheetah, Palimali, lying at their feet. They were holding hands. This I was happy to see; I'd talked many times about settling down with them in a cottage in the countryside, where they could feed me my meals and make sure I got everything I needed. I had meant to live there with Ta'ra, until that fairy Ta'lon had stolen her away from me. I'd decided instead that I'd allow Esme to live in our cottage.

Alliander and her troop of White Guards clearly needed time to reinforce their spell, and I could see from the expression on Aleam's face that he had a plan. Because of that, I wasn't as worried as perhaps I should have been. Although I still didn't like the secret Salanraja was hiding from me.

Not wanting to think too much about it, I strode over to Rine and Ange.

"Thank you for the save," I said. "I really didn't know you were coming."

Rine chuckled and tossed his mop of hair around his head. "If you did, would you have baked a cake?"

"You know full well that cats don't do baking," I replied. "But I could have served you up a hairball."

Rine shook his head. "No thanks. Think I'll stick to cake."

"I would too if I were you."

Ange laughed, then knelt down and tickled me under the chin. I chirped my appreciation. She always smelled of catnip, which is one reason why I liked her so much.

"It's just good to know that you're safe and okay, Ben," she said.

I considered telling them that I wasn't okay, that I kept hearing the voice of *Cana Dei* in my head. I decided it was better to keep quiet.

Soon after, the lights died down from the White Mages' staffs and the unicorns' horns. Alliander called out an order and they lowered them in unison. The wall behind us stretched up high, getting lost within a thick layer of mist that seemed to be part of the spell.

"*Can't you just fly over that?*" I asked Salanraja. "*You could pick us up in your claws and carry us away to safety.*"

"*It's a dome over our heads. We can't fly anywhere. Can't you see the top?*"

I turned my head to the side slightly. "*No,*" I said.

"*Must be a matter of perspective. Anyway, it's a method White Mages use to contain rogue dragons and other flying creatures. It takes a lot of magic to serve this up.*"

"There's a lot of White Mages," I said.

"*True that ... true indeed. Anyway, this is a time for diplomacy,*" *not for wild escape plans. If you'd heeded that earlier none of you would have got into this mess in the first place."*

"But we did use diplomacy," I said. *"We even enlisted the help of the king to retrieve our staffs."*

"What? King Garmin helped you?" I felt the shudder running down Salanraja's body as if it were my own. *"The problem is dire indeed ..."*

I really didn't know what Salanraja was talking about. *"Not King Garmin,"* I said. *"Rex, the King of Cats in Cimlean City."*

"The King of Cats is not the King," Salanraja said.

"Yes he is."

"No, he's not."

"He is – all the cats think so. At least the ones in his colony, anyway."

"Really? So what's the population of his kingdom?"

I bowed, meekly. *"Well, about sixty cats."*

"A mighty kingdom indeed," Salanraja said, and I could hear the laughter in her voice.

⚜ 33 ⚜

THE GAME OF DIPLOMACY

We waited and waited, the White Mages not talking to the dragon riders and the dragon riders not talking to the mages. This, I guessed, was part of the game of diplomacy humans liked to play. I decided not to interfere.

I looked over at Esme, surprised that she hadn't tried to be a part of this. But she was asleep in the grass – clearly not in a fighting mood. Max also had lain down next to her. Surprisingly, they were curled up close to each other. It seemed that Max and Esme were starting to get along.

Once Alliander seemed satisfied that the spell to summon the magical dome over our dragons was complete, she cantered forward on her unicorn, Tanni.

"Stand down, Driar Aleam," Captain Alliander said, looking down at him haughtily. "This is a matter for the White Guard."

Aleam shook his head. I couldn't see his face from where we stood, only the remaining strands of his grey stringy hair. Whiskers, it was good to see him healthy again. Last time I'd seen him he'd been recovering from a sickness so bad I could smell it in his sweat.

"Great Driar," Aleam replied. "You'd do well to remember that, Captain."

Captain Alliander scratched the back of her neck. "Your title doesn't apply here. We agreed back at Dragonsbond Academy that these students would be under my jurisdiction. I caught the cat summoning *Cana Dei*, endangering us all. Gracious demons, none of them are in any condition to go on a heroic mission right now."

Aleam lowered his head. "I know too well what happened," he said.

"And you have nothing to say about it?"

"Yes, I do actually," Aleam said, and he raised his head again. "You need to shut down every single tower in that city, and you need to do it now."

"And why would we do that, Great Driar Aleam? If it weren't for these towers we wouldn't have been able to track these insolent students across the country."

I yawned. These discussions were so boring. Esme lifted her head and blinked twice at me slowly, and Max stirred then made a soft snoring noise that soon became a growl.

"You did so because they were summoning *Cana Dei?*" Aleam asked.

"I did so because they used magic," Alliander said. "But once Initiate Seramina started using dark magic, the mage towers lit up. We knew her location to a pinpoint."

Seramina was standing close to the magical dome-wall thing. She looked as if she were trying to shrink in on herself, her elbows as close to her body as possible. Her staff had been placed on the ground in front of her. Alliander hadn't asked her to put it there, but she had done so anyway.

Aleam looked at her for a moment, then turned back to Alliander with his hand placed on his chin.

"So the problem, I hear, is that the students have started hearing a voice in their heads which they identify as *Cana Dei*. It seems to be blocking off their connections to their dragons."

Alliander nodded. "This is nothing new to me," she said.

"I'm sure it isn't," Aleam said. "But what is the source of *Cana Dei*? Where is it coming from?"

"Their connection to dark magic, of course," Alliander said.

"No," Aleam said. "It's not just our dark magicians here who are hearing the voice. Normal dragon riders are also hearing it, and I wouldn't be surprised if some of your White Mages aren't hearing it, too."

Alliander frowned. "Do you have proof of this?"

Rine nodded and stepped forward. "I heard it in my head when I entered the city," he said. "It told me to leave and not to rescue my friends. Fortunately, I didn't listen."

"I heard it too," Ange said. "At first I thought I was going mad."

A shudder went down my spine. I'd been told once that the magic dragon riders use is a type of dark magic, just that it doesn't use *Cana Dei*. But what if it could turn all dragon riders into dark magicians? What if it could consume their souls, just like it had with Arran and almost had with Seramina? I didn't like the sound of any of this at all.

Alliander's eyes narrowed. "How did you learn of this?"

"Through agents of the dragons posted throughout the city. And before you ask who, we're choosing to keep that information confidential."

"But it changes nothing," Alliander said. "They still broke the law."

Aleam's face went red and his nostrils flared. For the first time ever, I thought he was going to lose his temper and shout at Alliander. Perhaps he'd even draw his staff and call down lightning from the sky. But instead he took a deep breath and collected himself.

"Alliander, just listen to me," he said. "You have a serious problem which you need to address right now. *Cana Dei* has invaded Cimlean City. The Grand Crystal at Dragonsbond Academy has told us of great danger if you don't ramp up the guard and try to work out what's going on."

"But we've seen no evidence of this in the King's Crystal."

"*That is because* Cana Dei *has invaded the city.* It's skewing the magic there, and you need to put your resources into working out what is actually going on."

Alliander looked over her shoulder at the glowing walls. Could it be that Aleam had managed to break through her tough facade? Could he actually be changing her mind?

"What about the students?" she asked, after a moment.

"I'll deal with the students," Aleam said, "because I have need of them for something. Trust me. They're much safer out here than in Cimlean City right now, even in the School of the White."

Alliander looked over her shoulder once more, then she raised her staff and muttered something that was foreign to me under her breath. Salanraja and my crystal had granted me the ability to understand the languages of all living creatures, but that didn't include the language of crystals and magic.

A golden spark shot out from her staff towards the barrier that had imprisoned our dragons. It fizzled, and then winked out.

"There's one more thing," Aleam said. "The time is coming for us to act, and we need to act fast. Olan has already spoken to King Garmin's dragon, and we need to mobilise an army faster than anyone has ever mobilised an army before. We might need to fight in the next hour or two, so make sure your White Mages are readied."

Alliander frowned – the kind of frown which asks, "Are you serious?"

But Aleam's expression didn't change, and so the concern on

her face deepened. She called for her White Mages to quickly disperse into the city.

As soon as Alliander had turned her unicorn around, Lars spun to face Asinda, and she threw herself into his arms.

CAMPFIRE

The last of the unicorns disappeared behind the gates of the city just as the sky lightened to announce the coming of the new day. Soon afterwards, the walls of Cimlean City stopped glowing. The city seemed to lose its radiance, and the walls had a certain griminess about them. The domes of the magical towers no longer shone like polished gold.

The sky filled up with a layer of solid grey, and I guessed it would soon get cold in the city. We weren't cold, though, because we were sitting around a campfire. No one mentioned what Aleam had said about the army. It was clear to everyone that things were about to get dire, and for the moment we all wanted to enjoy being reunited. I guess we had all acknowledged that things were about to change pretty fast.

Ange was sitting with Rine, and Asinda with Lars, on a single log. Both young women had their heads resting on their partners' shoulders, staring into the flames. I lay down at the end of the log next to Esme, and we were doing exactly the same.

That's the thing about fire – it doesn't care what kind of creature you are. It hypnotises. Less intelligent creatures like ants, moths, and flies charge right into it. For them, fire is fatal.

Smarter creatures like cats, and those who are a little less smart, like humans and dogs, instead get sucked in by the display. Once you start watching the dance of the flames, it's hard to turn away.

What was even more mesmerising was the scent of the mutton sausages that drifted out from the spit above the flames. It was strange, because earlier that evening we'd hosted the greatest feast of sausages ever known to cats. But Rine, Ange, and Aleam hadn't eaten any of that meat, and nor for that matter had the dragons. It was a dragon rider tradition to eat mutton sausages on every single mission.

Of course, I wasn't complaining.

Seramina was doing the honours of turning the spit above the fire. Max sat beneath Seramina, more interested in the fat dripping from the sausages into the flames than in the fire. Aleam watched Seramina for a moment. He then looked at each of us in turn, and he let out a heavy sigh.

Seramina turned her head toward him. She didn't have her staff strapped to her back. Rather, it lay on the ground exactly where she had set it down when Alliander had arrived.

"What is it, Driar Aleam?" she asked.

Aleam lowered his head. "Your dragons have told me a lot about the situation – but I haven't told you what we've seen in the Grand Crystal yet, and I am afraid to do so."

Seramina's hand dropped from the spit. Esme shot up from beside me and rushed over to him.

"Is Bastet okay?" she asked. "We're too late, aren't we? I knew we were going too slowly. That's how *Cana Dei* managed to escape into Cimlean City, isn't it?"

Aleam shook his head. "I cannot answer that question reliably," he said, "but I do know that Arran is in the city, using the power of

Cana Dei and the lesser dark magicians who operate in the shadows. He's using them to open a portal from the Seventh Dimension to the Fifth. Soon the demons will flood in."

Esme hissed at him. "Why didn't you tell Alliander to try and stop him?"

"Because the Grand Crystal has shown us enough of the possible futures to see that they cannot face Arran without perishing."

"But you just told them to shut down the magic."

Aleam looked down at her and frowned. "That magic would only have accelerated the process. The truth is that the four of you need to go to the Fifth Dimension and help Bastet. You must go, and you must take your dragons."

My ears perked up. Aleam was one of the people who cared about me the most. I leaped down from the log and joined Esme in rubbing against his leg.

"Why not you?" I asked. "Why not Ange, and Rine, and Lars? Why not King Garmin's Dragon Guard or Alliander and her White Guard? Why do we always have to do this alone?"

Aleam scratched behind his ear. "Because of the crystals – they've shown us all the possibilities."

"You mean the Grand Crystal?" Esme asked. "What did it show you?"

"Just talk to your crystals," Aleam said. "Close your eyes and focus on them, and you will see the truth."

Whiskers, I'd forgotten about my crystal. But then, I guess if *Cana Dei* had indeed taken over Cimlean City, I wouldn't have been able to talk to it, just as I hadn't been able to talk to Salanraja.

I sat down, closed my eyes, and I entered the place that linked magic and dreams.

A thousand futures flashed before my eyes. Each one involved a gigantic portal that linked the First Dimension to the Fifth Dimension. Some involved the King's Dragon Corps leading the vanguard; others showed Alliander and other captains of the White Guard charging through on their mighty steeds. Some more revealed the fairies coming to our aid, Prince Ta'lon darting around casting magic as Ta'ra led other brave Cat Sidhe over the realm.

All but one involved magic blazing and demon dragons tearing down from the sky upon our allies. All of them caused thousands – some tens of thousands perhaps – to perish in battle. I saw my friends – Rine, Ange, Seramina, Asinda, Lars, and Aleam, lying on the ground, their eyes lifeless. Esme gone. Ta'ra gone. Salanraja gone. Not even the greatest of them all – the descendant of the great Asian leopard cat – survived.

But then there was one future that emerged out of all of these. It involved Seramina, Asinda, Esme, and I, flying our dragons through the darkness in the Fifth Dimension. That was all I saw. There were far too many future threads tangled together for the crystals to predict what might happen next.

In my mind's eye, I saw a great bright light before me, and that light faded to show my crystal – a tall, faceted thing spinning above the ground. It pulsed as a voice emerged in my head. It had a soothing Welsh accent, much more endearing than the dry and lifeless voice of *Cana Dei*.

"You walk in the shadow of the darkest force of nature. Draw its attention, and it will see you. Imagine it, and its great evil eye will turn upon you and bring destruction. But equip yourself with trust, furnish yourself with the courage to sail uncertain seas, and you will be invisible to Cana Dei. *This is what you must do, Dragoncat, and the four of you dark magicians must go to the Fifth Dimension alone."*

It made sense, I guessed. But I still didn't quite know how I would escape the notice of *Cana Dei*. Nor did I know how we would get to the Fifth Dimension in the first place, or what we would do when we got there.

"*Trust,*" my crystal said. "*This is all about trust. Keep faith in the future, and things will turn out how they are meant to be.*"

I guessed that was the best we could hope for. Because if Arran destroyed Bastet, if *Cana Dei* found its way into the other realms, we were all doomed.

"*Now open your eyes, Dragoncat,*" my crystal said. "*For your destiny awaits.*"

The light flared intensely bright in my vision. It forced my eyes open.

I was no longer at the campfire with my friends. Instead, I was surrounded by a velvet sky and a dimly-silhouetted landscape – its features limned with pink light. A shadow passed over me, and there came a high-pitched screeching sound from the sky.

35

PEP TALKS

There are only two forces that can move things between dimensions without the use of portals. The first is the magic of Capitut's Key. The second is the crystals themselves. And it was the crystals that had really got under my fur.

"Whiskers," I said. "You could have let me eat my mutton sausage before you sent me to the Fifth Dimension."

I was addressing my crystal, but I still said it out loud so everyone could understand my plight. I yowled it at the top of my voice. Then I made a deep growling sound and shook myself as violently as possible to try and purge my rage.

The motion calmed me down a little, though I was still seething inside. There came that screeching sound from overhead again – another aeriosaur passing by. The bat-buzzard creatures were here to protect us. They wouldn't attack us unless we intended to harm the realm.

I sniffed the air. The scent of snowdrop perfume wafted over from Seramina nearby. Behind it, the smells of the land weren't unpleasant; rather, they were redolent of fresh grass and honey. But that didn't change my mind about not wanting to be here.

Seramina stood in exactly the same place as before, but this time she wasn't behind a fire. Asinda was sitting on something which wasn't a normal log anymore. I couldn't tell what it was – everything here was so dark, and you could only identify objects through the patterns of pink phosphorescence that passed over them. Seramina's staff had also been transported here. It lay on the ground a short distance away.

Esme strode over to me and looked me right in the eyes.

"Didn't you eat enough in Cimlean City, Ben?" Esme asked. "We had mutton, and we had whitebait."

"Yes, but the cooking made me hungry again."

Esme let out an amused chirp. I heard a sniffling sound and turned to see Asinda wiping her eyes.

She met my gaze. "Lars ..."

My heart sank, and I felt bad. I might have been angry, but right now she was probably wondering if she'd ever see him again. She didn't need to hear me yowling my head off. She needed empathy.

"We'll go back to him," I said. "Our crystals showed us that this was the only way."

Asinda stood up and brushed dirt off her clothes. "You're right. We have to make sure we survive this."

"Still, we didn't have a choice in the matter," Seramina said, sounding lost. "Aleam told us to talk to our crystals, knowing this would happen ... and what was all that about an army?"

Esme went over to the young teenager and stared up at her. The Abyssinian was awfully energetic, given that we'd just been propelled towards our doom against our will.

"What?" Seramina asked.

"You've been moping for too long, Initiate Seramina," Esme replied. "And I'm sick of you dragging everyone down."

Seramina narrowed her eyes. "Well, I did almost destroy every-thing back at the Altar of Lore."

"And now you have a chance to save it," Esme said. "It's down to us now. So pick yourself up, and pick up your staff while you're at it."

Seramina's jaw dropped. Then she shook her head hard and walked over to her staff. She bent down to retrieve it. "You're right, Esme. We need to take responsibility – we need to do what we can."

"Glad you're seeing sense," Esme said, and rubbed her nose against Seramina's calf.

Whiskers, even though Esme's pep talk hadn't been meant for me, I also felt better about the situation. I hadn't played the hero for a quite a while and now I had a chance to be one again. Though admittedly, it seemed odd not to have Max here with us. Since our adventure retrieving Capitut's Key from the Calimar Desert, he'd always seemed to come along for the ride.

"Warg!" a voice suddenly said next to me, startling me. "Flying bat-buzzard-like wargs!"

Max had appeared out of nowhere. The ankh symbol branded into the fur on his side glowed bright red and faded. I snarled at him then told him off in the dog language. "Max, you're not meant to be here. You'll ruin everything."

"My crystal told me to come," Max barked back. "It said Max can help. It said good doggy, Max."

"Great," I said.

"You don't want me here? I bring you mutton sausages and you repay me like this."

Esme strolled over to us and brushed against Max.

"Of course he wants you here," she said. "You know Ben – he just gets a little anxious sometimes."

She moved away from Max, and came back up to me. She touched me on the nose. I felt calm all of a sudden. For a long time

I'd thought that the only cat who could bring me comfort was Ta'ra, but now Esme had proved a suitable companion. I guessed this was just how it was meant to be.

I turned to check that my crystal had kept its word about our dragons. It was a little hard to see shapes that were further away through the darkness of the Fifth Dimension, but they were there all right. Our four dragons – Salanraja, Hallinar, Shadorow, and Gratis – stood craning their heads about in wonder.

I guessed they hadn't been to other dimensions as much as we had, and they certainly had never been to the Fifth Dimension. Until recently, very few had even known what or who inhabited the land.

Camouflaged against the darkness, Corralsa was almost unnoticeable where she stood between them. The jet-black beast used to be Arran's dragon, but she and the Warlock Prince had never bonded, apparently. After Arran had snatched Max from the Fourth Dimension, just as Astravar had snatched me, Corralsa had ended up bonding with Max, the Sussex spaniel, instead.

There came another one of those terrifying shrieks from above. For a brief moment I saw a massive shape in the darkness, before it drifted out of sight. Not so long ago, the evil warlock Astravar had summoned the aeriosaurs into the First Dimension and hypnotised them into attacking Dragonsbond Academy. Impervious to anything except dark magic, they make formidable foes.

"I guess Arran hasn't opened the portal yet," I said.

"If he had," Asinda said, "we'd be hearing about it up there. The aeriosaurs are there to defend this place, remember."

"Then when will Arran attack?" I asked.

None of my friends answered my question; they didn't need to. Because above us the largest portal I'd ever seen suddenly appeared and stretched itself out over the sky.

Through it, the demon hordes swarmed in.

36

DEMON SWARM

Red clouds billowed out of the portal to the Seventh Dimension that now stretched across the sky. Streaks of crimson lightning tore through the air.

There came the cries of thousands of beasts of terror, and booms like rock breaking in two, like earthquakes rending the ground apart, like that crashing you hear in the worst of your nightmares, before you jerk up in your sleep and realise that nothing had made a sound at all.

I stared in horror at the demon dragons, demon albatrosses, demon pterodactyls, and all the other flying demons that were bearing terror down upon this land. They all had one goal, and I knew it well: they were here to find and destroy Bastet. And in turn that would end us all.

Our allies the aeriosaurs shrieked and charged at the invaders. Everywhere I looked I could see shapes crashing into each other, silhouetted against the raging red clouds. I couldn't see any of it up close, but I could imagine the talons and claws streaking across the sky, each beast trying to tear its enemies apart.

But both sides were apparently impervious to normal damage, which meant this battle would last an awfully long time.

Another wave of beasts came out of the portal. These ones didn't soar out, but instead plummeted to the ground. There must have been all kinds of demons there – from rats to crocodiles to hippopotamuses.

Then there came the sound of a thousand demon foxes yipping *Ride of the Valkyries*. Whiskers, the tune had really caught on since Arran had taught it to them. But where was he in all of this?

I twitched my whiskers. He might already have found his way to Bastet. She could already be dead for all we knew.

I'd been so stunned by the emergence of the portal that I'd missed Asinda's command for all of us to run for it. My friends were already halfway to their dragons.

"*Bengie, get over here now,*" Salanraja said.

"*Ben,*" I corrected.

"*This isn't the time. Just run as if your life depends on it.*"

I squinted at the cascade of demons, trying to work out how far away they were. "*I think it probably does.*"

"*Exactly, now run!*"

More waves of demons fell from the sky. There were creatures so massive that they looked like tiny meteors. My legs still felt frozen to the spot. Another wave of creatures crashed down, these ones looking like demon elephants, their tusks shining against the velvet sky. They hit the ground so hard that it shook, spurring me into action.

My legs were already aching from all the walking and running I'd done before. But I made it over to Salanraja's tail. I scrambled up onto her back and took my place inside her corridor of spikes.

This looked a bit like an elephant's ribcage sticking out from each side of her back and arching upwards. Before Salanraja had bonded with me, the humans had wanted to cut her spikes off so they could install a saddle. Salanraja had told me many times that meeting me had been the best thing that had happened to her. I'd apparently saved her from a fate worse than death.

Salanraja flapped her wings and we lifted off. I kept my ears perked up, listening to the screeches of the aeriosaurs and the even more terrifying roars of the demons. We turned away from the portal, heading straight towards the roiling darkness.

"Do you know the way?" I asked Salanraja.

"Corralsa's leading."

"She always leads," I said.

"That's because she's the biggest of us and the easiest to see."

I climbed up my dragon's neck and perched myself on her head so I could get a better look.

"How can you see her? She's almost the same colour as the sky."

"Because we're dragons," Salanraja said. *"And we have superior vision."*

"Superior to who?"

"To you, it seems. Now let me concentrate."

"Ah, so it is difficult."

"Just shut up, Bengie."

"Just trying to provide some entertainment to lighten the mood," I said.

The hills below were still black, but on top of their pink rims they also had a red glow to them, making them look like they were on fire. The scent of honey that had pervaded the air had been replaced by that of sulphur. There wasn't any sign of rotten vegetable juice yet, fortunately, which meant that *Cana Dei* hadn't entered the realm. But if we didn't move fast, it soon would.

Seramina flew to our right on her charcoal dragon, Hallinar, who was almost as difficult to see as Corralsa was. Still, Seramina's pale hair made her easy to see, though sometimes it looked like she was floating on thin air. Asinda was our left, on another charcoal dragon known as Shadorow. Again, her red hair seemed to dance in the light. Esme rode another black steed – the dwarf dragon, Gratis.

It was so strange. Salanraja was the only dragon here painted in vivid colours. Her ruby body now looked as rich as the sky behind us. In the light coming from the Seventh Dimension, her scales seemed to let off an ethereal glow.

We flew for a while longer before I saw pink lights set into a wall. Their reflections glimmered off the water that flowed beneath them. This was known as the Wall of Souls. Set into alcoves, inside incredibly sturdy containers, were the souls of every living creature in all the dimensions. If *Cana Dei* got in, it would no doubt find a way to destroy them all.

I turned my head to study the river below. Directly beneath us, a long canoe bobbed on the water.

"*There's the boat*," I said to Salanraja. It had carried us to Bastet's lair when we'd last been here.

"*I don't think we'll be needing that now.*"

A narrow cliffside path led down to the beach where the canoe was moored. Lines of craggy creatures were streaming down towards it. We descended, and I saw the long snouts of the demon foxes.

They had piled up at the centre of the beach and were clawing at thin air, yipping loudly.

"*They can't get through*," I said.

"*Esme told Gratis that Bastet's magic is keeping them out.*"

"*What – how?*"

"*Wasn't it Bastet that banished the demon dragons to the Seventh Dimension in the first place? I'm sure she knows a trick or too.*"

"*So what about Arran?*" I asked.

"*No ...*" Salanraja said.

"*What do you mean, no?*"

"*She can't keep Arran away. Now let me focus.*"

We passed over the boat, and then I felt a shift in the air. All of a sudden, the air lost its smell of sulphur and the freshness of the land returned. But still, there was a whiff of something else looming.

Rotten vegetable juice, the smell of *Cana Dei*.

"*He's in Bastet's lair,*" I said. "*I can smell it.*"

"*Then we better move fast,*" Salanraja said.

She tucked her wings into her sides and dove downwards to gain speed, before opening them again to recover into a glide. The other dragons followed suit. We skimmed the surface of the water, sending out a stream of ripples behind us.

The island that Bastet inhabited lay just ahead. I could see her giant form on the shore, surrounded by purple mist. As we got closer, I worked out what had happened, though I had to squint my eyes to see.

Bastet lay there, lifeless and alone.

Arran had already attacked her and won. If anyone had been around to help her, they were no longer there.

37

SADNESS

Gratis was first to touch down on the island that was Bastet's lair, and Esme was lightning quick in sprinting down the dwarf dragon's tail. She scurried over to Bastet, keening.

Salanraja touched down shortly after, and I sprinted down her tail and over to join Esme. I brushed up next to my companion, providing the warmth and comfort I knew she'd need.

Bastet lay supine, her tapered black head facing us. Purple crystals lay strewn over the dark sandy ground around her. They'd had their magic sucked out of them and now they didn't even shine in the light. These could have been golems, manipulators, bone dragons, or any of the other magical beasts that Bastet would have fought.

There wasn't any sign of the other cats – Bastet's protectors – who inhabited this realm. Bastet had fought Arran and his magical creations alone.

Bastet's body was still warm, but she wasn't breathing. No heat or familiar smells came out of her mouth or nose. Her eyes were closed, and the circlet around her neck reflected the red light streaming down from the sky. I lowered my head to examine it, sniffing for evidence.

Bastet remained lifelessly still.

"There's no point, Ben," Esme said. "We've lost. Arran has the amulet."

"It's not ..." My voice trailed off.

There was nothing more I could say. Bastet's amulet contained Capitut's key. If Arran had stolen that, then he could use it to grant the ability to exist between the worlds to anything he wanted to.

I ran my nose down Bastet's fur, tracing the revolting scent of rotten vegetable juice towards her stomach. I soon discovered a purple stain on her side, barely visible against her dark coat. Arran's magic had burned right into her.

I growled, watching the stain for a moment. It was slowly spreading outwards, like oil filling out the surface of a pond. In time it would cover her whole body, and after that happened I guessed Bastet would be dead.

"I can't heal it," Esme said. "Arran used the darkest of all possible magic – both white and dark magic will only make it worse."

I turned to see Asinda and Seramina hovering nearby. They both had their heads lowered, their hands folded at their waists. Max crept forwards and examined Bastet's lifeless face, then turned up his nose to howl to the sky.

There were no words in his cry, only sadness. It had a slight tune to it, sending out a sorrowful dirge across the land. A cold breeze brushed over my paws, stirring the sand beneath. I listened to Max's howl for a moment, then I tossed back my head and joined in. Esme looked at me, her eyes vacant. She lowered her head and rested it against Bastet's cheek.

"If her magic fades, then the demons will be able to move in," she said. "This land will be lost, and that also holds true for our souls."

I brushed my nose against her cheek. "I know it's not just about the souls, Esme."

She turned to me and blinked. "Bastet was …"

She had no words. I understood; I had no words either. It seemed like none of us did.

I turned away from her dying body, unable to watch anymore. I could sense it – the magic was fading around us. All along the wall that ran next to the river, the lights coming from the souls within their containers seemed to be dimming. Both Asinda and Seramina had tears in their eyes and neither of them tried to wipe them away.

I turned back towards the river and waited for the worlds as we knew them to end.

I had no idea how much time passed …

The shapes came out of the darkness like shadows emerging at sunrise. Some of them swam through the river, others appeared from out of the caverns in the rock that surrounded the beach. Some even seemed to come out of the sand itself.

Cats of all shapes slinked into view, miaowing softly. They edged along the sides of the beach, keeping close to the water, approaching slowly and cautiously. Every set of eyes was fixed on Bastet. Pink light reflected off them as they moved.

My hackles shot up along my back. I turned my head between each of our visitors, hissing and yowling.

"You left her," I shouted. "You could have fought, and instead you left her here to die."

"Leave them, Ben," Esme said. "They were only protecting themselves. They couldn't have fought Arran."

But that didn't stop me hissing at them. Still, they paid me no heed as they stalked past me. Rather, they were fully focused on Bastet. They had come to pay their respects.

The first cat stepped forward. She was a fluffed up Ragamuffin, younger than the old Ragamuffin I had grown up with back home. The cat leaned down and licked at the purple stain with her long tongue. It glowed pale blue as she did so. Wisps of blue smoke seemed to seep out of her long white fur.

More cats closed in, and they also started grooming the purple wound. Their tongues glowed the same pale blue as they did so, and that strange blue smoke drifted out of their fur. The air was slowly tinged with a smell like incense. But it was only faint.

Bastet didn't stir. She still wasn't breathing.

"What are they doing?" I asked.

"They're giving up some of their life force," Esme said, her blue eyes gleaming.

"Why?"

Esme didn't answer. Rather, she also stalked forwards and ran her tongue over the wound on Bastet's flank. At first I shuddered. That stuff *smelled* bad enough – I couldn't imagine licking it.

Esme's tongue glowed blue like all the others. That same blue mist seeped out of her fur, and it drifted towards Bastet and settled over her like fog settles over cold water.

Blue dewdrops emerged one after the other on Bastet's fur. They sparkled through the darkness. I took a deep breath as I realised that Bastet needed my help, too. I went over and also contributed to the communal grooming.

Together we groomed Bastet for a long time, not letting the warmth run out of her. Though she wasn't breathing, we could all feel her lifeforce. And I say we, because every single cat there formed a bond during that terrible night. I could feel the heat of hundreds of bodies huddled close to me. I was sweating through my paws, but I didn't care.

We licked at the darkness to stop it spreading over the mighty Bastet, as we would lick at bowls of milk. Unlike the best of such bowls, this disease that Arran had seared into her flesh tasted rotten. But it didn't matter; Bastet was our mother. We weren't going to let her die.

Hours passed, and in lands other than this one the sun would have wheeled up high in the sky. The ground continued to tremble, and the roars of distant battle continued to cut across the sky. The demons wanted to instil terror in us. They wanted us to give up. But not a single soul here did so.

Eventually the work was complete and not a speck of darkness remained on Bastet's shiny black fur. We all sat back and waited. We were exhausted, and every one of us wanted to sleep, but we didn't grumble or groan.

I remembered who I was that day – I wasn't just a Bengal, descendant of the great Asian leopard cat and the mighty George, but I was a cat among cats. I shared a moment of silence amongst my kin. Though the moment was short, it seemed to last for an eternity ...

Then Bastet opened her eyes.

❦ 38 ❦

ARRAN'S PLAN

Bastet's eyes blazed like molten balls of amber. She lifted her head, made a deep and loud groaning sound, and collapsed against the ground again.

"Bastet!" Esme shouted.

She sprinted over and licked Bastet's dark nose.

I stepped back, to see Bastet open her eyes again. She opened her mouth and looked at me, mouthing a single word.

"Dragoncat," she said.

My heart skipped a beat. Bastet had noticed me first, but I couldn't be proud, could I? Not in such a sensitive moment.

"Over here," Esme said, her head held high.

Bastet's gaze drifted over to her.

"Esme?"

Esme purred loudly as she lowered her head and touched her nose to Bastet's. "I'm here, Bastet. It's okay ..."

Bastet shuddered. She tried to stand, but as soon as she put weight on her front legs they shook vigorously, and she fell to the ground again. She glanced down at her side, then her gaze tracked downwards towards where her amulet should be.

"He took it," she said. "Arran has the key."

Max barked, as if he understood. "Evil smelly old master!"

"Max," Bastet said, and her soft, deep voice didn't just resonate through the air but imprinted itself on our brains, for everyone present to hear.

She was speaking the cat language, but she was also speaking the dog language and the human language, too. I don't know which language her mouth uttered; it didn't matter with Bastet. What mattered is that everyone understood.

Seramina stepped forward and touched Bastet's side where the wound had been. She rubbed the fur there as if she were stroking a normal cat, not the great giant who was three times the size of her.

"I never thanked you for saving me back at the Altar of Lore," she said. "Now I'm happy to see you're alive."

Bastet's purr was loud enough to create waves. "I'm immortal, aren't I? As long as the cats believe – as long as we stay brothers and sisters and help those in need, then I shall live."

"But the wound?" I said. "It looked like it was about to kill you."

"And yet you all came to my aid," Bastet said. "Such is the nature of destiny. Fate is far more determined by our choices than we realise."

She put weight on her hind legs and gently managed to lift herself up on them. Her front legs still shook as she raised herself, but she managed to stand on them. When she locked her stifle joints, she stood as tall as a small house. The circlet around her neck reflected the light from the distant souls, shining brightly as they should again. But still, something was missing. Her medallion no longer adorned her chest, and it made it look rather odd. Bastet now looked like a regular cat – albeit a giant one – wearing a golden collar.

Something else was missing too; it seemed awfully quiet around me. I spun around to see that the cats had left us. They'd returned to their cubby holes to leave us alone to talk.

"Did you order the cats away?" I asked Bastet. "You did, didn't you? And you told them to hide when Arran was here. You fought him alone on purpose."

Bastet's yellow-eyed gaze went distant. "Had I not, they would surely have perished."

She looked down at one of the dead purple crystals and brushed it aside with her paw.

"But maybe you could have stopped Arran," I said.

"Ben …" Esme said.

I wasn't listening, but growling instead. "They should have fought for you, Bastet."

"No," Bastet said. "They shouldn't have … he brought the worst enemy of cats with him. If they had fought it, they would surely have died."

"Who is *it*?" I asked.

Esme shuddered. "Cerberus …"

"Who?"

"A hellhound of the worst sort," Esme said. "A three-headed giant dog of the Seventh Dimension."

Now it was my turn to shudder. I'd already met and battled a demon Maine Coon that had called itself 'Hellcat.' I'd somehow defeated it in chimera form, but not without the help of Lars' magic. A demon three-headed dog sounded much, much worse.

"Great," I said. "So we not only have to deal with a mortal enemy of cats, but Arran has your amulet with Capitut's Key inside."

"And yet," Bastet said, "you still haven't learned what Arran plans to do with it. You still don't realise what's at stake."

"What do you mean?" I asked.

Bastet looked down at Esme, who had her pink nose turned up towards her mentor. "Tell them, Esme," she said.

"Esme?" I asked her.

Esme turned to me and then looked away. Her gaze went distant.

"*Cana Dei* told me. It talked to all of us, I know – it tried to take over our minds. But I tricked it. I made it think that I was under its control."

My hackles felt as sharp as porcupine needles on my back. Esme kept telling me she was my companion, but she was also incredibly good at keeping secrets.

"Tell me," I said.

Esme looked up at Bastet.

"Go on," Bastet said.

Esme took a deep breath. "If Arran gets what he wants, then it will end us all in an instant. Because he plans to use Capitut's Key to brand *Cana Dei*."

A cold shiver ran down my spine as the realisation washed over me. This was much, much worse than I'd thought.

39

PURPLE VERSUS WHITE

Before I'd met Max and learned that Arran was evil, Capitut's Key had been secured in a sealed pyramid in the Calimar Desert. Except it wasn't just in the Calimar Desert – the pyramid existed in all seven dimensions, including the Sixth Dimension which linked the dimensions together.

Capitut's Key granted the ability to enter the Sixth Dimension, which allowed one to go to whichever dimension one pleased.

And, given *Cana Dei* was technically a lifeforce that powered all magic, branding it with Capitut's Key would instantaneously allow it to exist in all dimensions. No one would see it coming; it would seep out into all the worlds, sucking the lifeforce out of anyone who didn't serve it.

Those sleeping in their beds would sleep no longer. Those watching the moon outside at night would suddenly collapse to the ground. Rex and his colony of cats would slide down from the roofs, as pigeons plummeted around them. Unicorns would no longer smell of horse but of rotten vegetable juice. Each of the seven dimensions would be consumed by permanent darkness, becoming silent and lonely places.

"That's it," I said. "All hope is lost."

"No, there is still hope," Bastet said.

"How so?"

Bastet snapped her head towards me. "Why do you think I summoned you here?" she said. "Why do you think I spoke to the crystals and had them send you?"

I growled. "That was you?"

Esme walked over and brushed her head against my shoulder. It calmed me a little.

"She did the right thing, Ben. You know that."

"But why is it always us?" I asked. "We're just two—" I looked at Esme "—one regular cat, a dog, and two teenagers who should be living normal lives. Whiskers, I should be lapping up milk and feasting on smoked salmon in South Wales. The only things I should have to chase after are butterflies."

Bastet crooned softly. She lowered her head to me so I could smell the fish right on her breath. She smelled of salmon, I could have sworn it. Before she'd planned this, she'd had a bowl of smoked salmon just to tick me off.

Asinda stepped forward and turned her harsh gaze down upon me. "Don't you think you're a little out of line, Ben?"

"No," I said. "No, I'm not. For almost a year now we've been serving the whims of the crystals, and what have we gained for it? We've been thrown around between dimensions, we've been locked up in a school with smelly unicorns, and even my companion—"

I glared at Esme.

"I lost my companion," I continued. "I lost Ta'ra. And maybe it would have been better if I'd never met her, or any of you, or my dragon. Life would have been so much easier, and I don't deserve any of this. None of us do."

The silence which ensued was so thick that I could have scratched it with my claws.

After a moment, Salanraja said in my head, "*This is very hurtful. I hope you really didn't mean what you said.*"

"*I don't care what you think, Salanraja,*" I replied.

"*Do you mean that?*"

"*Will you just get out of my head!*"

She did exactly I asked. Or I blocked her out, I guess. She had warned me never to block her out, but I did.

Another voice emerged, smooth and dry, yet comforting. I felt a burning sensation behind my eye sockets. Yet it didn't hurt – rather, it filled me with power.

You can have whatever you want, Dragoncat. Join us, and anything you desire can be yours.

I looked around. Five set of eyes were staring at me. But only Bastet's showed compassion. The rest showed abject shock. Then I noticed Esme's staff-bearer looming above her. The Abyssinian held her staff in her mouth.

"It's taking control of you, Ben," she said. "Don't let it, or I will be forced to stop you."

She thinks she can take you, the disembodied voice said. *But she can't. I can show you how to defeat them all.*

I don't know where it came from; I don't think I willed it to do so, but my staff-bearer appeared out of thin air, and plunged my staff into my mouth. Energy came from somewhere, and purple mist rose around me. Purple light glowed in the crystal at the end of my staff, filling my mouth with a raw, burning sensation.

"Ben," Esme said, and she started to circle me. "Push it away. Control yourself!"

I could see Seramina and Asinda at each corner of my eye. They both looked frozen to the spot and unwilling to fight me. But Esme would.

Purple light flooded out of my staff, and it concentrated into a focal point where it met a beam of white magic coming from Esme's staff. There was a bang, then a fizzle and a shudder.

I felt powerful. Energy surged through me, filling me with joy. Flashes of all the great food I could be eating passed through my mind: bowls of smoked salmon, roasted duck, spiced lamb, and other delicious feasts all laid out on a wooden table before me.

You have more power within than you've ever realised, Dragoncat ...

I narrowed my eyes and focused on the glowing sphere of energy that pulsed where the two beams met. Magic coursing through my veins, I willed more into me, and I became drunk on the power.

For a moment I thought that I would have it all. I would take down Esme, then I would turn my magic to destroy the rest of them.

Max was there, standing beneath the beams, barking. He wasn't going to let me do this, and I could hear him saying it in the dog language.

That was when I saw it – in slow motion, he prepared himself to pounce.

Let it be ... destroy them all. Otherwise, they will destroy you.

Whiskers, I was going to kill Max if I didn't do something. Maybe I didn't deserve all of this, but Max deserved it even less. As far as being innocent went, he was the most innocent of us all.

He leaped, heading right between the beams. Whiskers, they would sear him in two.

The idiot!

I cut off my beam, and Esme's white magic hit in me in the chest. I went rolling over the ground. My head hit something hard and I saw stars.

Soon afterwards, I blacked out.

40

WITH THE FISHES

Y *ou could have had it all ...*

The voice filled me with shame. I was worthless, power-less. I deserved to die. But I wasn't dead yet—

Fish spun around my head through the darkness. I watched them as they floated, in all kinds of different colours. Had I not gained the gift of every language, I would not have known the names of them. But as I focused on each one, I found myself calling them out in the human language in turn.

Zebra fish. Clownfish. Angler fish – with big scary dangling light. Trout. Pike. Swordfish.

Forget about the fish, Dragoncat. What matters here is your soul.

Behind the fish, the darkness floated. It buoyed them up, and it didn't take me long to realise that the fish weren't in fact swimming. Rather, the darkness was propelling them to where it wanted them to go.

Flying fish. Minnow. Whitebait.

Stingray. Dogfish. Great white shark.

Strangely, I wasn't thinking of eating any of them. I wasn't a cat in this place; I didn't know what I was. Part of me wanted to join them in the darkness. In the distance, I saw a school of salmon. I belonged with them. I had swum with them in other places, other dreams.

Embrace the darkness, Dragoncat.

The water – the darkness that surrounded me – had neither heat nor chill. I lifted a fin, and I realised I was just like these creatures, ready to swim obliviously through the dark water. My life, my goals, didn't matter to me. What mattered was the current that was buoying me along.

It could carry me forever through the darkness, and I wouldn't need to worry about anything. The darkness would preserve me, keeping me safe forever, so long as I submitted to its will.

Once again, I studied the school of salmon in the distance. Their names didn't matter – I was a part of them now. Swimming towards oblivion; swimming towards safety, complacency, and not needing to do anything for myself ever again.

I swished my tail, moved my fins, angled my body to direct me through the current. I only needed to find the right angle. The darkness would carry me the rest of the way.

A voice came, disembodied, through the darkness. It barked like a shark bite.

"Ben! Ben! Don't become a warg!"

Ignore it. All that matters is the flow. It should be easy – no need to resist.

It *was* easy. Bubbles rose around me. Swirling within the darkness, even darker than the rest of it, was a spinning orb. Tendrils snaked out of it and then dived back into its surface. Like tiny little fish emerging from the water.

This was it. Destiny. The current would take me where I needed to go.

Suddenly there came a rush of bubbles. It hit me right in the face, sending me reeling backwards. My face felt warm, then cold. But that wasn't right. There was no temperature in this place. I didn't need it anymore.

A voice. Familiar.

"I'll help you! My friends can't be wargs!"

That is resistance you hear. Keep swimming, my loyal fish. Embrace destiny like the rest of them. Be one with your shoal.

Resolute, I closed my eyes and carried on forwards. I had a purpose here. It was the only place that I'd ever had a true purpose. Something to achieve.

Something hot and wet slapped my face. More bubbles came, followed by a rush of warmth, then a chill.

Another voice came, deep and growling. A female voice, soothing and kind.

"Bengie, there you are. I can see you. Gracious demons, don't get lost in there."

I knew that voice.

"Salanraja?" I asked. *"Salanraja, are you there?"*

Ignore it. There is no place for her here. You only need me.

"Salanraja?"

Silence. But the fish were still spinning around me, and ahead my shoal was getting away. I beat my tail, letting it propel me through the water. I moved fast and the current shifted me towards my destination. Soon I was with them, safe and secure. A part of the crowd. Born to conform.

"Ben ..."

"Salanraja?" I jerked myself to a halt, spinning backwards.

"I know you didn't mean what you said, Ben."

There was another voice – thin and reedy like a teenage girl's.

"Come back to us, Ben ... I know what it's like. Look for the light."

Then came a richer voice, again female, laced with passion. "Ben, you must fight it. Don't give in."

Ignore them, said *Cana Dei.* I knew it for what it was now.

I was dead in the darkness. My body had gone limp, and salmon crashed into me from all directions. Each collision pushed me forward, and I tumbled unthinking through the current.

It would be so easy to give in. I just needed to let go.

"I don't have the strength," I said, and I didn't just say it here, but also on another plane.

Which is why fighting is futile.

Then there came another voice. This time, it spoke in a different language. It was feline, laced with command, yet elegant.

"Use compassion, Ben," Esme said from somewhere nearby.

"What?"

Ignore her ... you cannot wi—

"Compassion. Turn the darkness upon itself."

"What do you ..."

I swivelled my eyes downwards. I saw my scaly fish snout, and the length of wood that my teeth had clamped onto. Unlike the staff I had grown used to, this didn't have a purple crystal stuck onto its end.

They weren't in focus, but they didn't need to be. Along the staff's length bright crystals glowed, like magical barnacles sticking to a branch.

The last voice I heard in that dark place sang with a lilt and had a Welsh accent.

"This is the final gift we will give you, Dragoncat," my crystal said. *"From now on, you will need to learn how to use your gifts alone."*

I could feel the power building in the staff. But this time it didn't burn my muscles, nor did it fill me with a lust for power. Instead, it brought a warm and fuzzy feeling.

The feeling that I was doing something good.

Use compassion, Esme had said.

And I did. I imagined all of the hardships that I'd seen along my travels. I forgot about my imagined hunger, and I forgot about everything that I had ever wanted. It was the first time in my life that I had actually cared about everyone else. Really cared, I mean. I didn't care what they might give me. I cared what I could give to them.

The staff glowed, and *Cana Dei* screamed within my mind. Yet it had no voice anymore.

An explosion of white spread out from my staff, and I opened my eyes into the real world – the Fifth Dimension – with conviction that everything was going to be okay.

We were going to find a way to win.

❧ 41 ❧

GUARDIANS OF THE WHITE

Asinda, Seramina, Esme and I stood surrounded by a circle of cats – Bastet's helpers had returned. As our staffs glowed white, they fed them with energy. White columns rose up into the sky from each one and converged into smaller arcs that fed our staffs with magic.

Bastet had planned this all along. That is the way of immortals; they play humans and cats and dogs like pieces on a board. But I didn't mind, because she'd saved me, and in doing so, she'd also saved her friends.

Now I understood where Esme got her magic from. While regular White Mages had their unicorns, she sourced it from this realm, and the cats here donated it to her.

Did they give up their lifeforce for Esme's magic, as they had to heal Bastet? I didn't know. But I did know that now they weren't going to use their powers to help Esme only, because three more of us had gained Esme's power of the white.

My staff wasn't the only one that had transformed. Seramina

and Asinda also had lost their purple crystals. Instead, their staffs had white crystals glowing along their lengths.

Through facing *Cana Dei*, it seemed, I had brought us close enough to harness its power. All I'd needed was some allies, and that was why the crystals had sent the three of us to this realm. It was the only way to save us from the inevitable future *Cana Dei* had planned for all dark mages.

Esme's, Seramina's, and Asinda's eyes were glowing white. Their crystals also glowed with a similar brightness, four spheres of magic spreading out from each staff, including my own. I guessed my eyes looked much the same, but there was no mirror to see myself in, and the water that divided us from the Wall of Souls displayed no reflections.

Our dragons stood behind each of us. Salanraja wasn't talking to me, but she didn't seem angry. Rather she understood that I needed to concentrate. I still had my staff in my mouth, and I was somehow casting magic out of it. In all honesty, I didn't know what the whiskers I was doing but it definitely felt good.

The spheres we were casting met in the centre between us, where a bright orb of light glowed. It looked just like the orb that Esme had cast back at the School of the White. Spirals of *Cana Dei* leaped out and back into it.

The air was filled with a pleasant warmth. Our magic seemed to sap away the stench of sulphur coming from the distant portal. I could hear the howls and roars of the battle, but it now seemed so far away.

Bastet looked down from high above us, her eyes filled with approval. Max was standing next to Bastet, looking comically tiny next to her massive paw.

"Not fair!" he said. "Not fair! When will I get my staff?"

"In time, you too will play a part," Bastet said. "But for now you must join the battle against Arran. Together you can defeat him – it is not yet too late."

"But Arran has the key," I said. "I know I'm not to lose hope and all that, but we've still been given an impossible task."

Bastet's gigantic whiskers twitched. The air shimmered between them.

"Arran hasn't yet gained the ability to open my amulet," she said. "And the only way to do so is to harness the power of the void."

I remembered what Lasinta had told us. The only way to kill an immortal was to send it to the place from where it cannot return. But he hadn't needed to steal Bastet away to do it; he'd only needed to grab the amulet and leave her weakened enough to get away. *Cana Dei* would have finished her off when it entered this dimension. It had all been a part of the plan.

"I guess when you say the void," I said, "you're talking about the Eighth Dimension."

"Nothing but," Bastet said. She turned her head towards the river. The pink caps on it showed clearly the direction it was flowing. "The Soul of the Worlds flows from its source to a waterfall known as the Final Falls that connects the river to the void."

"The Soul of the Worlds?" Asinda asked.

"That's what we call it. The rock upon which you stand has a soul, and it exists across all the dimensions. But even worlds will one day die. Their souls will eventually dry up. It will all eventually come to an end."

I shuddered. I didn't like the sound of that at all.

"Relax, Dragoncat," Bastet said, turning to me. "It will take many millions of years for that to happen, and during that time many generations will pass. So long as *Cana Dei* doesn't come here, that is. Because its true purpose is to close the void. Like every living thing, it fears death."

I focused on the white ball at the centre. I hadn't yet worked out its purpose, but I was feeding magic into it. Our collective minds were telling us exactly what to do.

"I guess to do so, it must first inhabit this world," Seramina said. "And its only way in is through Capitut's Brand."

"You are truly great for a such a young mind," Bastet said. "The portal to the void is like the crystals. It exists in all the worlds. As does the Soul of the Worlds, right up to its end at the Final Falls. In all dimensions except this one, it is underground. *Cana Dei* can only close the portal by filling out across the worlds. You know full well what the consequences of that would be."

"Total annihilation," Asinda said.

"Every single soul extinguished," Seramina said.

"No more salmon," I said. "Ever, ever again."

Bastet lowered her head so that she was level with us, and stretched out her paws on the black sand. "Now you know what's at stake. The only way to open my amulet against my will is to feed it to the void. Then if Arran is quick enough he can reach out and snatch back the key."

"And as soon as he does so, he can take it across the dimensions," Esme said. "He can go to the ghost realm and brand *Cana Dei* within seconds."

Whiskers, it put me into a rage thinking about it. "We need to stop him," I said. "How do we know he's not already there?"

"Because he still has to travel the river," Bastet said. "While you can get there instantaneously."

"But how?" I asked.

Bastet's gaze drifted towards where the river disappeared into the darkness. "I can use the magic of this place to banish the demons back to the Seventh Dimension, but it will take time. I cannot do it until I am fully healed. Your allies – and their army – meanwhile are already waiting at the Final Falls. They must protect you from the demons so you can go after the Warlock Prince."

Come to think of it, Lasinta had also mentioned that Bastet had the power to banish anyone from the Seventh Dimension. It was Bastet who had sent Apopis, Ammit, and the other demon overlords to the Seventh Dimension in the first place. I guess it made a lot of sense.

"There's just one thing that doesn't make sense," Seramina said, her hand resting on her chin.

"What's that?" Bastet asked.

"If you can banish any creature from this place, why didn't you banish Arran as soon as he got here?"

"Because he has Capitut's Brand," Bastet said. "He can stay in this dimension because of it."

Asinda bent down and picked one of the dead crystals up off the ground. "I guess that's how he managed to get his magical creations here as well. The crystals can exist in every dimension, right?"

"Exactly," Bastet said. "I can't banish them here without banishing them from all the dimensions. To do that would mean that magic could never exist, which would also mean I couldn't cast the magic in the first place."

"This is giving me headache," I said.

"Exactly," Esme said. "You can't magic away a paradox."

"So how much time do we have?" I asked.

"I do not know," Bastet said. "Healing cannot be rushed, and so you must have faith in the future."

"But what if you can't?" I asked. "What if you don't heal in time?"

"All I can tell you is that more than one possible thread of the future ends in your victory. You must now have faith that you can win. Because if you don't, you're almost certain to lose."

"The unknown," I said. "*Cana Dei* and the darkness. It's such a scary place."

"It is," Bastet said. "Still, it's better to embrace the unknown than to cower in the dark. Those who don't remain forever lost."

"But if Arran is already on the way to the Final Falls, how can we get there in time?"

"We'll get there like this," Esme said, and she closed her eyes. Both her staff and the orb in front of us glowed brighter for a moment. A shockwave pulsed out of it, washing over me and pulling back my fur.

"Farewell, brave magicians," Bastet said, her voice getting fainter. "You are now my Guardians of the White."

And just like that, our magic teleported us right to the Final Falls.

The spell took our dragons and Max with us. As Bastet had promised, most of our allies had already arrived, and the biggest battle I'd ever experienced was about to commence.

42

WHAT A BIG ARMY YOU HAVE

The spray where the Final Falls met the void glowed, sending a soft, warm light across the darkness. It cascaded down into a long drop that ended far below us. What with how violently the waterfall was crashing into the dark pit, it looked like it should emit a roar, but the effect was muted. Even sound couldn't escape the void.

In the distance, the portal to the Seventh Dimension still billowed with red clouds that raged crimson lightning. The demons had stopped swarming out of it, but some hidden part of me – perhaps the part that was connected to the magic – could feel them approaching. Every bristle in my fur was standing on end.

Another portal gaped through the darkness, this one much closer to us. It led into the First Dimension, and our allies were almost through. Everywhere I looked, I could smell fear – or at least the chemicals associated with it. It was present in the horses, the unicorns, the humans, and most of the other beasts that had joined our army. I could just imagine everyone's hearts beating hard as they waited. My heart was pounding too. None of us knew what was coming next.

The only creatures I couldn't smell fear on were the dragons. Somehow they seemed resilient against terror.

Captain Alliander and a good dozen other White Mage captains formed the left side of our army, their troops all mounted on their unicorns, staffs at the ready. They had called upon all kinds of magical creatures associated with white magic.

Phoenixes, wisp dragons, and griffins beat their wings into the sky. Chimeras and some kind of cross between a badger and an armadillo lined the ranks in front of the unicorns. White Mages hadn't summoned these creatures from other dimensions, but had called upon them for aid. Against Arran and his demon army we needed all the help we could get.

King Garmin's Dragon Guard took the rightmost flank. Lars was at the front, together with a line of shield mages – all of them with white crystals upon their staffs and mounted on dragons of different colours.

Asinda had taken Shadorow around so she could spend time with Lars. Her charcoal mount and Lars' citrine dragon, Camillan, now stood side by side, and both riders had their heads turned towards each other. They weren't saying anything, just gazing into each other's eyes in the way that loving humans do, their pupils dilated.

Now the regular troops were making their way through the portal. If it hadn't been for all these magical creatures and mages, it would have looked just like a regular army. I used to see armies like it in historical dramas on the television. Back in those days, I had wondered why humans liked to watch people run around in armour, clashing their swords and shouting at each other. They could instead have changed the channel to one of those nature documentaries, which I thought were much more entertaining.

We had a row of riders on regular horses. Nothing magical about them. Behind them, the men carried very sharp-looking pikes. Then there was a row of swordsmen, and two rows of archers spanned the rear. Still there were more troops that needed to come through the portal, after which the White Mage standing near the back would be able to close it.

I recognised that White Mage to be Carmista, and she turned to look at Asinda before shaking her head with a gentle smile on her face. I guessed she realised that we were right all along to try to escape the School of the White.

The students of Dragonsbond Academy had also joined the fight, but they stood right at the back behind the regular Dragon Guard.

I could see Bellari – Rine's ex-girlfriend and my ex-nemesis – on her citrine dragon, sidled up next to a handsome-looking teenager. Rine and Ange were on the other side of their squadron, just behind our superiors – the Council of Three and Aleam upon their mighty dragons, Aleam sitting on the great white Olan at the front. Palimali – Ange's cheetah from the Sahara Desert of the Fourth Dimension – was strapped in with Ange on her sapphire dragon, Quarl. Honestly, I wondered if she wouldn't be better off helping the beasts who were supporting the White Mages. But wherever Ange went, Palimali went with her. They had the same kind of bond that I seemed to have developed with Max.

Seramina, Esme, Max and I were right at the centre of it all. We sat upon our dragons, ready to lift into the sky. Our job was simple, and perhaps the most difficult. We hadn't even needed to meet with our superiors to discuss it – the Council of Three's dragons had debriefed our dragons, who in turn had debriefed us.

Simply put, if Arran reached the Final Falls and harnessed the power of the void to obtain Capitut's Key, then it was all over. We had to stop him; we had to bring him down.

"*It's an impressive sight, don't you think?*" Salanraja said.

"*What, the army or the waterfall?*"

"*Both.*"

"*Well, the army is big, and the waterfall doesn't have salmon leaping up it. Once it does, I'll be impressed.*"

"*Nothing can leap out of the void, Bengie, you know that. That's why it's called a void.*"

"*So what happens if we get sucked in?*"

Salanraja hesitated. "*I really don't know. I guess we cease to exist. Let's not think about that, shall we?*"

I turned back to look at the waterfall. We weren't the only ones staring at it; this was the first time most of our ranks had been to the Fifth Dimension. Before we'd battled Astravar and his aeriosaurs, very few had actually known it existed.

I turned back towards the horizon ahead. A red line traced across it, filling up with clouds of brimstone. Soon we would see the first demons charging forwards. I perked up my ears and listened for the sound of the *Ride of the Valkyries* yipped out by the foxes that I imagined would lead the charge.

"*Are you scared, Salanraja?*" I asked.

Salanraja turned her head upwards and to the side. Her great yellow eye swivelled around to look at me.

"*You know, in all the time I've known you, I think it's the first time you've asked that question.*"

"*Well, I used to be too afraid to ask it. The first time I tried to talk to you, you sent a jet of fire over my head.*"

"*That's because you tried to steal my venison.*"

"*I didn't know it was yours.*"

"*Still, don't you naturally protect your food? I've heard you scream at Ta'ra before for stealing your mackerel.*"

I had nothing to say to that. Salanraja had an annoying habit of being right about most things.

"*Anyway, I'm not afraid anymore,*" I said. "*Not since I discovered the secret behind white magic.*"

"*But you are scared, Ben, I know you are. You forget that I can read your feelings. But you don't seem able to read mine.*"

"*I can ... I just don't feel the fear in you.*"

"*No, you don't hear the fear in me, because I ignore it; I don't acknowledge it. But that doesn't mean it's not there.*"

I twitched my whiskers. "*What do you mean?*"

"*My fear resides in that burning pit that dwells even deeper than dragonfire. Without it, I would lose my soul.*"

I lowered my head. I could smell the sulphur, and I could feel the heat pouring out of the distant portal to the Seventh Dimension.

"*Fine, I'm scared,*" I said.

"*I know. You let the fear shout at you in your mind all the time.*"

"*Then how do you stop it?*"

"*You don't,*" Salanraja said. "*You just need to let it be.*"

I thought about that for a moment; *Cana Dei* had taken advantage of me because of my fear. It had almost consumed me, like it had almost consumed Seramina.

"*Thank you,*" I said to Salanraja.

"*For what?*"

"*For being so wise,*" I said.

And for once I meant it. I had paid my dragon a compliment, and it worked, because it caused Salanraja to croon. Then she turned her head back to the emerging army, and the slight elation I'd sensed inside her drifted away.

43

DRUMBEATS

We must have spent another half hour filing into ranks and making sure everything was in order. I watched the troops shuffle into different positions, listening to the shouts from the lieutenants, captains, and commanders who ordered them to move. After a while I realised how boring it all was.

On television, they never show the hours and hours of preparations before one of these battles. At least it gave me time for a good grooming session. My fur by this point was absolutely filthy and tasted both of sulphur and rotten vegetable juice.

Eventually there came a crashing sound from the portal, startling me out of my trance. An orchestra of percussionists were arranging themselves at the back of the regular troops. Several of them rolled a bass drum as big as a building through the portal. A line of drummers followed, carrying snare drums that they beat as they marched into line.

Once in place, the bass drum joined the percussion. Every minute that followed, its boom filled out over the landscape, keeping us alert. The snare drums followed in a regular rhythm – once per second.

Boom-da-da-da-da-da – the sounds went, on and on. Then, just after I thought I'd got used to all the *das*, there came another *boom!* It made it impossible to fall asleep. The inside of my ears was hurting so much that I had to keep them flattened against my head. As the drumbeats continued, Asinda blew a kiss to Lars and then flew Shadorow over to join us. She belonged in our unit – the Guardians of the White.

"What are they doing?" I asked Salanraja.

"Keeping time."

"And why would they need to do that?"

"Because we need some way to measure the minutes."

"Is time that important?" I asked. *"Don't we just charge when we see the enemy?"*

In all my life I'd never needed to measure time to achieve anything. Back in South Wales, the only regular event that had determined my life was my mistress calling me in for food.

Salanraja chuckled under her breath. *"Of course time's important. It helps keep the archers in sync, and tells the catapults when to fire. It will allow our commanders to coordinate the troops with utmost efficiency. Also, the demons will latch on to it, and they'll follow the drums like wasps towards honey."*

"You mean to say that we're luring the demons towards the regular soldiers first?"

Salanraja lowered her head. I felt a deep rumble underneath my paws, coming from her chest.

"Sadly," she said, *"we have no other choice. Our best defence against the demons is for the White Mages to outflank them."*

"And what about the demons that fly? The demon dragons and the like."

Salanraja sighed, sending out a plume of smoke ahead of her.

"You do realise that we can't kill the larger demons, don't you?"

"I brought down a demon dragon once," I pointed out.

"Yes, and the magic knocked you unconscious for hours. Look, it's simple. Our army needs to lure in the bigger beasts while the White Mages and Dragon Guard work on the smaller ones."

I guess it made a lot of sense. Once Bastet gained enough power, she'd be able to banish all the demons from this realm. The only thing was, we didn't know when she'd get strong enough to do so.

Boom! Boom! Boom! Boom! Boom!

There came five beats of the bass drum in quick succession. It startled me so much that I almost slipped off between Salanraja's spikes.

"What was that?" I asked.

"They're here," Salanraja said.

Boom! Boom! Boom! Boom! Boom!

Honestly, I'd never heard something so loud. It was even worse than a demon dragon's roar.

To my right, the dragons opened their wings and lifted themselves up into the sky. To my left, the White Mage captains shouted out orders in unison. All of the white mages raised their staffs, and both these and the unicorns' horns glowed a bright white.

The archers raised their bows, arrows nocked. The swordsmen beat their shields with their pommels. The cavalry turned their horses to the front.

Boom! Boom! Boom! Boom! Boom!

"Let's get a better vantage point," Salanraja said. She spread out her wings and launched us into the air. Corralsa, Gratis, Hallinar, and Shadorow followed suit. We quickly formed a line above the regular army.

A purple line of dust had started to rise on the horizon, and a red cloud quickly bloomed over it. The demons and Arran's magical creations were no doubt behind this.

If I listened hard enough, I might be able to hear the yipping of *Ride of the Valkyries* from the demon foxes, who took the front line. But the *da-da-da-da-da* of the snare drums below made me unwilling to raise my ears.

Boom! Boom! Boom! Boom! Boom!

One final beat, then the drums fell silent. There came a loud fizzing sound, then the portal to the First Dimension closed, sealing us in.

Shortly after, there came a loud shout from the rear of the army.

"Archers! Nock! Draw! Loose!"

⚜ 44 ⚜

CHARGE!

The arrows sailed up through the dark sky. They reached the top of their arc, twirling. The smells of sulphur and rotten vegetable juice edged closer.

As Salanraja hovered in the sky, the four dark dragons around me, I kept my ears perked up. If something happened, I wanted to know about it.

Just before the arrows could fall, Captain Alliander shouted out another command to the White Mages.

"Magic!"

Thousands of magical beams shot out from the unicorns' ranks, setting the arrows alight. They glowed as they fell. The horizon filled with white fire.

The sight was spectacular. It was like watching fireworks but without all the noise.

"Archers, ready!"

Boom! Boom! Boom! Boom! Boom!

Again, I flattened my ears against my head.

"Nock! Draw! Loose!"

The archers launched another volley of arrows. The White Mages cast their magic, and once again the horizon blazed white. In the distance I heard whimpers and shrieks. I guessed the archers had managed to wipe out some of the demon rats. Though, if Bastet had asked her cats to join the battle, we could have done so ourselves.

Still, it didn't stop the charge, for soon afterwards I heard the thundering of hooves. These weren't normal hoofbeats. They didn't sound like the dainty plinking of unicorn hooves either.

They belonged to thousands of demon creatures. Demon horses and zebras and wildebeests, and anything else the Seventh Dimension wanted to throw at us, and they were coming in fast.

I couldn't see their rocky edges through the darkness. What I could see was their glowing molten cores beneath the cracks in their stone skin.

"Cavalry! ... Charge!"

Our horses were spurred into action. They whinnied, flared their nostrils, flung back their rear hooves, then galloped into the fray. The black dirt of the Fifth Dimension kicked up behind them as they went. The lightly-armoured riders drew their sabres and yelled a battle cry.

As the horses charged onwards, the riders gripped their swords tightly. The demons and the cavalry clashed. Sparks flashed off the swords as they beat against the craggy monsters from the Seventh Dimension.

ROAAAAAAARRR!

That roar hadn't come from any of the beasts our cavalry was fighting. Those were the roars of demon dragons. The noises came so loud that it caused Salanraja's scales to shudder under my paws.

Our drums shouted their response.

Boom! Boom! Boom! Boom! Boom!

"Archers, ready! Nock! Draw!"

The cavalry wheeled back. As an organised unit, they charged back towards us. The demon cavalry tried to chase after them, but their ranks were too chaotic, and they ended up tripping over themselves.

"Loose!"

Another volley launched into the air, sailing over the horses that flooded back towards us. For the first time in my life, I respected those creatures. They were incredibly brave, doing exactly what their riders willed them to do. I still thought they smelled terrible, though.

Another beam from the white mages hit the line of arrows at the top of their trajectory. They looked like shooting stars as they fell back towards the ground.

"Ground beasts!" It was Alliander who'd shouted. "Charge!"

There came the roar of a hundred lions, the bleating of a hundred goats, and the grunt of a hundred badger-armadillos. The chimeras went first, driven by their hind hoofs whilst their front paws gathered strength to strike.

At the same time, the badger-armadillos curled up into balls, displaying tough-looking carapaces. At first they started at a slow roll, gathering enough momentum to eventually overtake the chimeras. They crashed into the demon swarm first, sending out a sound like boulder crashing against boulder.

The chimeras entered the fray soon after. I couldn't see what was happening, but I could hear the roars, the gnashing, and the snarls.

ROAAAAAAARRR!

It came again, so loud that it seemed to split the air apart. Our snare drums were still going, letting out their steady rhythm.

"*When do we join the battle?*" I asked.

I already had my staff bearer summoned. It hovered nearby, twitching, with my staff in its grip.

"*When did you become so eager to enter the fray?*" Salanraja said.

"*I want to try out my white magic,*" I said.

"*Just wait … you'll know when it's time.*"

I waited, squinting my eyes. The battle was too far away to see what was happening.

"*I wonder where Arran is,*" I said.

"*Trust me, everyone's wondering the same.*"

I knew what I had to watch out for: a demon dog with three heads. If Arran was anything like Astravar, he'd be riding it. I just hoped he wasn't riding a demon dragon instead.

Boom! Boom! Boom! Boom! Boom! Boom! Boom!

The demons were coming out much faster now, accelerating.

"Ready!" someone shouted, and the cry echoed down the ranks, repeated by the superiors.

The whole army roared in response.

"Chaaaaarge!"

We watched the soldiers surge forward.

"*Now is the time,*" Salanraja said.

She flapped her wings and we started moving.

DECOY

Our army charged forwards in one organised motion.

The pikemen and swordsmen screamed as they ran. The archers dropped their bows and took out swords of their own. The cavalry, meanwhile, had split into two. We'd been told that they would try to outflank the enemy.

The whole strategy was an attempt to stop Arran from getting through.

The White Mages let the regular troops get ahead, then fanned out behind them. They cast all kinds of magic over their ranks. I hoped that the spells would keep the soldiers safe. I also hoped they would stop the demons in their tracks.

We just needed enough time for Bastet to cast her magic. Then, once we'd stopped Arran, everyone could go home.

If we *could* stop Arran, anyway. I was still uncertain about our chances.

The phoenixes, griffins, and wisp dragons stayed in front of the White Mages. The dragon riders formed a line behind them, staying in the air.

But we didn't go in that direction. Instead, Salanraja and the four dark-coloured dragons headed towards the Final Falls.

"*Where are we going?*" I asked. "*The battle's over there.*"

"*That may be,*" Salanraja said. "*But we're meant to guard the waterfall. Arran has to get here eventually.*"

"*Why didn't you tell me this?*"

"*Because you would have moaned and asked questions all the time, and I just wanted a little peace and quiet.*"

I groaned under my breath. I turned my head to watch the battle growing ever more distant. Magical creatures had now joined the fray, including the golems.

Fire golems launched themselves from their distant places. They were a dangerous projectile weapon of the warlocks that would explode upon impact, incinerating anything that they touched.

Fortunately, the shield mages had taken the vanguard of the Dragon Guard. They shouted out something and pointed their white crystal staffs downwards. Protective magical bubbles shot up around our troops.

The fire golems hit the surface of the bubbles and exploded. Their flames licked over the shields like water. It burned the black grass for a minute. But the ice mages were quick to extinguish the most violent of the fires and the lightning mages called down storms which washed the remnants away.

There came a high-pitched shrieking sound, which was again familiar. The spindly forms of the bone dragons came into view, their wispy Manipulators feeding them with white energy from the ground. So long as the bone dragons had their hosts beneath them, they were invincible.

The battle whirled on as we wheeled around to the left. We headed towards where the foam of the Final Falls was hitting the void, oblivious to the cries and roars and shrieks from the battlefield.

I smelled smoke, I smelled dark magic, and I smelled more and more sulphur, as endless ranks of demons piled in.

Whiskers, how long was this going to last?

Seramina, on the back of her charcoal dragon Hallinar, shouted something. She pointed off to the left. There was something charging below us. It was a man with his red cloak billowing behind him as his mount barrelled forwards.

He held a staff with a purple crystal on it. His mount, just as I'd expected, had three elongated heads. It ran like an incredibly nimble hound, much more so than Max.

"*Gracious Demons, it's Arran,*" Salanraja said.

"*He sidestepped our entire army,*" I said. "*It was all a decoy.*"

"*Then we'd better go down and stop him.*"

But we didn't have a chance, because it seemed Arran had already spotted us. Or at least his magic, or the power of *Cana Dei*, had alerted him to our presence.

He spun Cerberus around and raised his staff above his head. Thousands of purple beams shot upwards, and then quickly curved back down in very tight arcs.

They hit crystals that had previously been invisible on the ground – or at least they'd been too far away to see. Now they were glowing purple, looking like stars against the dark.

More Manipulators arose, quickly summoning bone dragons into the air. Clay golems formed out of dark puddles in the ground. Shadowy shapes also found their way out of the darkness.

For a moment I had thought this was going to be easy. But now we'd been ambushed, and our army was too far away to help.

46

GROUND BATTLE

The bone dragons launched themselves towards us, sending out acidic purple flames ahead of them. Their hosts, the manipulators – wispy spectral beings – continued to feed the bone dragons with energy. Behind the army of magical creations that Arran had summoned, Cerberus with the Warlock Prince upon him raced towards the Final Falls.

I summoned my staff bearer, clenched my teeth around my staff, and called upon the unfamiliar white magic, ready for a fight. Unfortunately we needed to get through Arran's minions before we could even think of facing him. Salanraja stated the exact words that I dreaded every time.

"Bengie, you're going to need to fight them from the ground."

"Ben," I said.

"Gracious demons, will you stop correcting me during crises?"

"Just drop me off. I'll deal with them."

Salanraja roared and then dived towards the ground. The other dark dragons were already ahead of us with Esme, Max, Seramina, and Asinda riding upon them.

Shadorow dropped Asinda off first. She rolled over on the ground, recovered, and shot a beam of white magic at a manipulator. She hit it right in the heart – where the crystal that powered it was hidden. The manipulator vanished and the crystal fell to the ground.

Seramina jumped off Hallinar, and she cut a wide horizontal beam right across the landscape. It took out three manipulators at once.

Then it was Esme's turn. Gratis – being smaller than the other dragons – managed to get really close to the ground. He swept his tail downwards, and Esme stalked quickly down it in a brilliantly coordinated manoeuvre. She landed on the ground, her staff already in her jaws.

Two manipulators spotted her, and they both sent shots flying at her. They crisscrossed before they hit the ground, because Esme had already scrambled out of the way.

She let out a loud yowl as a sphere of white magic came from her staff. It spread out in a wide horizontal arc. Four manipulators disintegrated into dust and wisps of smoke, and four dull purple crystals fell to the ground. They spun there for a few seconds before coming to a halt.

"*Your turn, Bengie,*" Salanraja said.

"*Ben.*"

"*Just go!*"

I didn't have time to reply, because she'd already lowered her back and tail at such an angle as to send me hurrying down. If she'd done that a year ago I would have instinctively grabbed on to her scales with my claws. But I could see the bone dragon hurtling towards us.

Purple gas poured out of its faceted jaws. I managed to dive out the way before the acid ate me whole. Salanraja roared and soared up towards the sky.

The bone dragon went after her. But this was stupid, because Salanraja was deliberately luring it away. My dragon performed a loop-the-loop, allowing it to whizz past her. She came back down and sent out a jet of flame at its tail. Esme had already destroyed its manipulator, so it had nothing to protect it. It crumbled into ash.

With my staff clutched between my jaws, I focused on the battle ahead. Behind all of Arran's minions, I could see the three-headed dog and the Warlock Prince getting ever closer to the waterfall. We had so many enemies, and if we didn't get through them quickly, we were all toast.

Meanwhile Esme, Asinda, and Seramina were doing their best to cut through.

A beam whizzed past me, and something sprouted from the ground. Vines shot quickly upwards. A giant bulbous head emerged at the top of them. The mandragora had a mouth with sharp teeth, like a giant enraged Venus fly trap. It lurched down, jaws snapping.

I darted out of the way, and quickly scanned for the manipulator that had summoned this thing. The mandragora spat out dirt and came towards me for another bite. My body didn't know which direction to run towards. I was paralysed.

The jaws closed in. I saw darkness.

Suddenly and unexpectedly, a searing heat washed over me.

The fire had come from a dragon. The mandragora burst into flame and turned to ash.

Corralsa passed overhead, only visible against the darkness because of the flames below. She turned to the side, and I saw Max wasn't on her back. He must be on the battlefield somewhere. Or maybe he'd escaped momentarily into another dimension.

I didn't have time to think about it.

I turned back to the manipulators and cast a beam of bright white magic. This felt just the same as casting dark magic, except now I didn't hunger for the power. Rather, the act of casting healed and soothed me. I felt suddenly calm, and was able to focus on everything round about me.

All of a sudden, a puddle emerged beneath me. It had slithered over so slyly that I hadn't noticed it sliding under my feet. But now I could see the two crystals floating there – one red and one blue. They could only mean one thing.

I'd encountered a clay golem.

A massive hand came out of the puddle and clasped me around my waist. Up rose the rest of the golem, taking me with it. I was lifted metres into the air. Soon I was looking right into the red and blue crystal eyes of one of the very first magical creatures I'd ever faced.

I turned my staff towards it, but it twisted me to the side so the staff faced away from it. I angled my head differently, the beam spreading out over the landscape, hitting whiskers knows what. I needed to hit the red and blue crystals that made up its two eyes. But I couldn't get a track on the creature. Every time, it knew exactly which way to turn me in order to stay safe.

It tightened its grip around my waist, so much so that I couldn't breathe.

My body grew limp, every muscle giving out. My staff dropped out of my mouth and fell towards the ground.

47

RUN, KITTIES. RUN!

Breathless and wriggling within the clay golem's grasp, I heard the sounds of battle around me become ever more distinct. I could hear two battles, in fact.

There was the nearby buzzing of magic and roaring of flames. More distantly, there came the booming of the demon dragons, and the sounds of swords clashing against demon skin. Horses whinnying, chimeras roaring. Occasionally the bass drum boomed.

My ribs ached, and I was running out of air. My eyes had gone blurry. I couldn't see anything that was going on around me, but I could see the faint purple light given off by the mist that was caused by all this dark magic. A bitter smell of rotten vegetable juice pervaded the air.

"Ben, get ready to jump!"

It was Esme's voice.

But it couldn't have been. I must have imagined it.

There came a flash of white light, and then another. In front of me, the red and blue crystal – the clay golem's eyes – flashed brightly. Then they were tumbling, and I was falling. My spine twisted, and my natural instincts angled my feet towards the ground.

I landed with a soft thud. My vision came back, and I looked right into the bright blue eyes of Esme, my saviour. She wasn't holding her staff in her mouth.

Purple smoke rose from the ground where the clay golem had been.

My staff ... it was lying on the ground next to me. I moved to pick it up.

"Leave it to your staff bearer," Esme said. "There's no time."

"What?"

She turned her head towards Cerberus. Arran stood behind the demon dog. I could see his distant form leaning over the waterfall into the void, and something dangled from his hand, glinting in the light.

I glanced around quickly to assess our situation. Our dragons were still fighting the bone dragons, and we still had a lot of enemies to bring down.

"Whiskers, it's starting," I said.

"We need to get moving now."

She started sprinting, and I swore in the cat language under my breath. But it was a smart move. We were much nimbler than the humans. Much smaller. Much more likely to break through. I summoned my staff bearer. In one deft movement it swooped to pick up my staff and disappeared into oblivion.

I didn't waste a moment. I dashed after Esme.

We ran straight towards a row of manipulators. They turned slowly, sweeping their staffs around in a narrow arc. Beams came out of them, approaching fast. Static pulled on my fur.

For a moment I thought we were about to be fried. There was nowhere to turn.

Suddenly, two beams of magic passed overhead, spreading out in a broad line. The aim was perfect, and the manipulators were wiped out in an instant.

"You owe us one!" Asinda shouted.

"Go give them hell!" Seramina yelled.

I looked back to see the silver-haired teenager pump her fist in the air. I should have been looking straight ahead, because more mandragoras had sprouted up around us. Esme led the way, and together we darted through the tangle of vines. We were careful not to touch any of the plants, because their thorns were tipped with deadly poison.

Behind me, the mouths of the mandragoras bit at the dark earth. One got so close to my tail that it tore off a lump of fur. I yowled in pain.

But still, I continued on ...

Running for my life.

Running for Esme's life.

Running for Ta'ra's and all my other friends' lives.

Running for the fate of the salmon and the world.

Two stone golems stood guard at the end of the track. They had their hands raised, and they had seen us coming. Their single crystal eyes swivelled around the grooves on their heads, and I felt one of them looking at me.

Then, their heavy arms – thick as tree trunks – swung downwards. I could see we wouldn't make it. Not if we didn't speed up.

"Esme!" I shouted.

"Put everything into it!" she screamed back, and she didn't turn back to say it.

She lowered her head and gained momentum. I'd never seen a domestic cat run so fast. I needed to do so too.

I imagined myself as a cheetah. I pretended I was Palimali, sprinting through the Sahara Desert. If the Savannah cats had seen me that day, they would have been proud.

My legs moved like whirlwinds. Every inch of my spine was focused on propelling me forward at maximum speed. My thighs ached, and I could feel them burning. But I wouldn't, couldn't, stop.

CRASH! CRASH!

The stone golems' massive fists collided with the ground behind us. The earth shook. Had I been stationary, it would have knocked me over. But instead I let the quake propel me forward without stopping.

My legs ached. They cramped out.

There came a mighty barking from ahead of us, and I caught sight of slaver dripping from a massive beast's muzzle. Behind that head were two more, equally fierce.

Cerberus had been waiting for us, and he seemed angry. Both Esme and I jerked to a halt.

CERBERUS

We now faced the fiercest beast I'd ever encountered. I mean, demon dragons were scary. But when you saw a demon dragon, you tended to see it a long way away. They also didn't look as if they considered you their next meal.

Cerberus did. Every muscle in his three faces glowered and scowled. His teeth looked sharper than my claws when they'd been recently sharpened. Six burning red eyes glared at me.

It wasn't the kind of look that measured the weight of your soul.

It was the kind of look that said, "I will kill you next!"

A good twenty paces lay between us and Cerberus. With the way that the tendons were wound around Cerberus' four lithe legs, I knew he could cover that distance in seconds. He was also so bulky that he completely blocked the view of the Final Falls that roared behind him. Because of this, I couldn't see Arran.

Esme summoned her staff bearer. It plunged the staff into her mouth. She immediately charged it up.

I had a better idea. I willed power into my muscles. They tore and my joints popped. I yowled in pain. Soon my yowl became a mighty roar.

Within seconds, I was a chimera. I turned my snake head towards Cerberus and hissed. I saw the reds and pinks of the Fifth Dimension in vivid colours through the snake head's eyes.

Cerberus let out a growl that shook the earth beneath my feet. It didn't just come from one head, but three simultaneously. It made me wonder – did a beast with three heads necessarily have three sets of vocal chords?

Then he charged.

I caught a glimpse of Arran then. He still had the amulet held over the void. He was using his staff to summon a rift of purple magic above the pit that the waterfall plunged into. This was creating a vacuum that pulled golden flakes away from the amulet. Piece by piece, it was eating the amulet away.

A flash of white, a short beam, came from Esme's staff. It hit Cerberus on his central head, right between the eyes.

It hit him hard, but Cerberus didn't tumble backwards. Rather he ground to a halt, as if from his own volition.

The three heads snapped towards Esme, and out came that horrible growl again.

Esme let off another beam of white magic. This one lasted longer.

"You will let us past," she said. "Or you will die."

Cerberus seemed to have a different opinion on the matter. The beam continued to sear into him, but it didn't seem to hurt him. Fire gleamed through the cracks in the beast's rocky skin. A whiff of sulphur passed over me, so strong it almost knocked me out.

The demon dog charged at Esme, though the white magic slowed him. He continued onwards, pushing against the force of the magic. Esme's eyes became slits, narrowed in concentration.

I let out a bleat from my goat head, and a roar from my lion's head. Both were meagre compared to Cerberus' loud barks and bayings. I kicked back on one goat's hoof, and sped forward.

49

GOODBYE, DRAGONCAT

Cerberus loomed before me.

I tucked in my lion's head and lowered my neck so that the goat's horns were facing Cerberus. The Final Falls roared behind him. If I could knock the beast far enough ...

Patterns on the dark ground whizzed passed me. The pink outlines of the grain faintly resembled streaks of pink light. The sand gave way where my front paws touched. But my weight was on my hind hooves. They didn't falter over the terrain.

Cerberus turned his nearest head. He shifted his weight to his hind legs, getting ready to flee.

But it was too late. I was already bearing down on him.

I hit him on the flank. The weight of the impact shuddered down my body, twisting the muscles in my neck.

Cerberus was knocked backwards. He howled loudly. His cry resounded over the terrain, even more terrifying than the call of a thousand wargs. The rage of the distant battle responded with its own howl, as if the demons were communicating.

The demon dog teetered slightly, but didn't fall. I didn't want to stay in range, so I trotted away to the left. A sharp pain bit into my flank. Adrenaline flooded through my system, numbing my muscles and easing the pain.

My snake tail saw Cerberus lift its rightmost head from where I had been, its jaw wide open.

Whiskers, he had bitten me. Was he venomous?

I couldn't worry about that now.

"Just one more pass," Esme shouted. "I can hold it."

My side felt numb, and the numbness had started to drift down my right leg. But I needed to focus. I needed to carry on.

I wheeled around, my stamina coming from some deeper part of me. I considered calling my staff bearer. But I didn't have time. Each second lost was a second Arran could use to destroy Bastet's amulet. A chance for him to acquire Capitut's Key.

Somewhere within me, perhaps from the white magic, I gathered the strength to wheel around in a wide circle. I'm not sure how long it took. Each second was precious.

Esme now had her eyes closed, and the white magic streaming out of her staff flared even brighter. Cerberus' legs were facing towards her, pushing back. He didn't move an inch from his position, and from the tightness in Esme's face I knew she couldn't hold this forever.

Cerberus' necks twisted away from his body. His heads faced me, his jaws snapping in challenge.

I had to rely on my horns. I lowered them again, keeping my snake tail raised high so I could watch the terrain ahead of me. I accelerated, and I ran faster than I'd ever run before in any form.

Wham!

I collided with Cerberus, hitting him right on the hard palate of one of his mouths. I snapped my goat's head back before his jaw snapped shut. His head jerked backwards, and the momentum carried him towards the edge.

He teetered over slightly. His other two heads snapped at me, snarling. Esme's magic weakened, soon fizzling out. Six red eyes glared at me in intense anger. The chasm leading into the Final Falls yawned in invitation.

Cerberus' rear paw slipped first, and his body followed. He scrambled to keep hold of the edge, but he got caught in the flow of the waterfall. The Soul of the Worlds carried him down into the void, and the last I heard was a cry like the most mournful of dogs.

Esme collapsed to the ground.

I turned to Arran, ready to charge at him too. In this form, I could easily knock him into the void if I was quick enough, destroying Capitut's Key in the process.

He had a wide grin stretched across his face. He no longer held Bastet's amulet. Rather, he had Capitut's Key – the bejewelled ankh that gave the power to walk the dimensions – held up between the thumb and forefinger of his right hand. It glowed, brightly.

"Goodbye, Dragoncat," he said. "Welcome to the end. Everything now belongs to *Cana Dei.*"

Darkness grew around Arran, and he vanished into another dimension.

A moment later, I collapsed to the ground.

50

THE RETREAT

I lay on the earth in the Fifth Dimension, wanting to sink into it. A purple glow traced each grain of soil. Warmth rose up from it, reaching out, embracing me.

I knew I was useless in my chimera form now, so I willed my muscles to shrink back into my feline form. I was no longer a great Bengal – descendant of the great Asian leopard cat and the mighty George – I was merely a helpless animal with a throbbing pain in his side. My companion Esme lay weakened some distance away, far out of reach.

I had no idea how long it would take Arran to brand *Cana Dei*. Lasinta had claimed he could do it instantly, but maybe she'd been wrong or had lied to give herself better chances of spurring us into action.

My side was now throbbing, and the pain was spreading into my head. I felt so tired. So weak. I closed my eyes ...

Time passed ...

"Fall back! Fall back!"

The cries of a thousand voices snapped me back to awareness. I opened my eyes to see our army retreating. They were sprinting towards the void that had swallowed Cerberus. Behind them clouds of red and purple roiled, looming.

I smelled sulphur. I smelled rotten vegetable juice.

Our enemies had rounded up our army, and they were heading towards us. Whiskers, we had lost.

I closed my eyes again ...

A flash of light forced them open.

I smelled emptiness, as a black cloud started to seep out around me. It flickered between light and dark, as it tried to establish its place in this realm. Dragons passed overhead. I saw Quarl and Ishtkar – Rine's emerald and Ange's sapphire dragon – flying next to each other. I didn't know if my friends were up there or not.

Our army crowded around us, heavy feet treading the dark earth. They were getting ever closer to the void. Whiskers, the demons were trying to push them in. What had happened to the aeriosaurs? Had the demons defeated them? Maybe they weren't invincible after all.

Light, then dark. Another flicker of *Cana Dei.*

Oblivion. This was the end of it all.

"Ben ..."

A smooth and gentle voice.

"Asinda, that's Ben ..."

I turned to see silver hair, floating towards me. Seramina underneath it, with her staff held out. She rushed forward and leaned down to me.

"He's been hurt."

"Do you know how to heal him?" Asinda asked. She was running in beside Seramina. I couldn't see their faces, only their hair. Silver and amber. Two blurred forms against the darkness.

Seramina drew her staff. She turned it towards me. The pain

subsided. It felt like stepping out into the rain after rolling in the mud. My vision returned. I opened my mouth.

"Esme," I said.

Asinda's eyes widened. "Where?"

I turned my head towards where I'd seen her fall. Soldier's feet stood between us now. Edging backwards. Seramina's gaze followed mine.

"Go to her," Asinda said. "I'll look after him."

Seramina rushed off. I tried to stand up. My legs shuddered and I collapsed face first.

"Esme," Seramina called. "Esme, where are you?"

"It's not safe," someone said to her.

"Don't go that way. We're in retreat."

Seramina didn't listen. "Esme ... Mind your feet. Don't step there. The one you know as Magecat has fallen."

I tried to stand up again, managed, though my legs wanted to drag me back down towards the earth again. I called my staff bearer, willed it to bring my staff towards me. It approached slowly, finding its way through the crowd. Soldiers looked up at it warily.

"She's here," Seramina shouted. "Esme, are you okay?"

I turned back to Asinda. "Arran – he got away."

Asinda reached down and placed a finger under her cheek. She didn't move it. Her eyes were watching the sky. Looking out for someone. Lars ...

"Enemy in sight!" someone shouted.

"Form a shield wall!" shouted another voice, louder.

Then there came a roar from the front from multiple soldiers. "Turtle!"

My mind was getting clearer. My staff bearer placed my staff in my mouth. I heard a voice in my head.

"*Ben,*" it said. "*Ben, you're back.*"

"*Salanraja,*" I answered. Then, "*What's a turtle?*"

"The soldiers will lock shields. It's our last stand. What happened? You blacked out."

"We've lost. Arran ... we didn't stop him."

"Ben ..." Salanraja's voice trailed off.

Above the dragons had turned, hovering.

"Magic!" The cry came from the ranks. It was Alliander. She was out there somewhere. "Support the swordsmen."

I turned back to see Seramina's silver hair. She was pushing back through the ranks, finding her way to us.

Nestled in her arms lay Esme, her eyelids sealed tight.

COMEBACK

Darkness surrounded us. The ground still emitted a soft pink glow, but even that seemed to be fading. Crimson lightning flared out of the distant portal to the Seventh Dimension occasionally, but it did little to light our way.

Seramina placed Esme down beside me. I sniffed her white fur. She was warm; blazing hot and shivering. Still breathing, but faintly. Beside us, the battle raged. Behind us, the waterfall fell into oblivion, hissing like the spray of a faucet.

"I couldn't do anything," Seramina said.

I turned to her. "You healed me okay."

I still had the ache in my side. It wasn't debilitating anymore, but it was there.

"But Esme knew all the spells," Seramina said. "She was directing us all this time. Telling us what to do."

"We need her back," I said.

"What's the point," Asinda said, her gaze distant. "If you lost Arran, then it's over ..."

But I wasn't going to go without a chance to say goodbye to Esme. She at least deserved that.

"We must try," I said.

I clamped my jaw down on my staff. A beam of white magic emerged from it, spreading out over Esme. I didn't know what I was doing, but I had no intent of harming her. The magic seemed to shape itself to my will.

Seramina sniffled, then she lowered her staff towards Esme. Asinda did the same.

The beams from our three staffs met in the centre. There was a warmth, and for a moment I thought I saw a rainbow in the ball of magic we produced. Streams of *Cana Dei* still danced in and out of its surface.

Esme opened her eyes. "Bastet?"

I returned my staff to my staff bearer, then strode forward and licked her on the forehead. "Not Bastet ... Ben."

She looked at me, her eyes still distant from the fever. The sky flared bright, and then fell dark once more. *Cana Dei* would soon be here.

"Ben ..." Esme said.

I took a step back. "We lost."

Esme's eyes narrowed. Her eyelids looked heavy. I licked her on the nose to keep her awake.

"Esme," I said. "I wanted you to know—"

"No," she interrupted.

"What?"

"We've not lost. There's still Max." She stood up. She didn't look fit to stand, but she did. "We must be ready."

"Max? He's ..." I stopped to think a moment. "What can Max do?"

"Summon your staff bearer, Ben," Esme said.

"My—"

A giant hand appeared from nowhere. It plunged a staff into Esme's mouth. It came in so fast that I thought it would topple her over. But somehow, despite her trembling legs, she managed to stay on her feet.

Esme shot a beam out over the Final Falls. "Arran will appear there. Now get ready."

I growled, feeling once again that I'd been kept out of the loop about something. But Seramina and Asinda looked equally perplexed.

"How do you know?" I asked Esme.

"Bastet. Just trust me for once, Ben."

I guess I had no choice. I called upon my staff bearer. Then, with my staff placed firmly between my lips, I waited for Esme's call.

"Brace yourself!" came a distant shout from our ranks.

The dragons above me charged. An image of the battlefield flashed into my mind's eye, coming from Salanraja's mind. Demon dragons, and all the other aerial and ground demons were surging forward. Within minutes their army would push us over into the abyss.

With the Final Falls looming behind them, our allies had no choice but to fight.

"*Thank you, Ben,*" Salanraja said. "*For everything. This is now the end.*"

"*Just hold on there, Salanraja,*" I said.

She said something back, but I didn't quite hear it. My mind was focused elsewhere.

Because out of nowhere, there came a snarling sound. A dog growling out in its own language, "You're the worst warg of them all!"

A human form flickered into existence before us. Beneath him, a dog had its mouth clutched firmly onto his red cloak. The man – clearly Arran – was swinging his staff around, trying to push Max off him. The hand that wasn't holding his staff was clutched around a glowing object. Capitut's Key.

Arran and Max flickered out again, then back in, then out, then in.

Whiskers, who'd have thought? Max was pulling him back into the Fifth Dimension.

"Now!" Esme said.

A beam shot out of her staff. Two beams very quickly followed, from Asinda and Seramina. I cast a fourth, just as Arran and Max flickered back into this realm.

The beams hit Arran right on the chest. Time seemed to stop, as if we'd opened a portal. Arran turned his head around, his eyes wide in surprise, and Max, the brand of the key on his flank flaring brightly, let go of Arran's cloak.

Time sped up once again, and Arran stumbled backwards, his cloak whipping out in front of him. He tried to keep his balance over the edge, but he had his staff held out too far behind him. The weight of it pulled him out into the abyss, and he fell screaming.

The cry didn't linger, but was cut off, the void swallowing all possible sound.

Max peered down into the void. The ankh was glowing on his side, but then it faded.

Arran had been destroyed, and Capitut's Key with him. Now no one could walk the dimensions ever again.

But we hadn't won just yet …

52

BANISHMENT

The demons had had a bond with Arran, and with his demise they seemed to feel it. The war cries cut off for a moment, as the beasts of the Seventh Dimension readjusted themselves.

Any of his magical creations left in the enemy's ranks would have returned to their crystals. Still, we had a whole army here facing an army of demons who were now free to serve whomever they liked.

Eventually they roared, and screeched, and their hands and hoofs and paws and feet banged against the earth, shaking it violently. Troops were still crowded close to us, and I could smell the fear everywhere. The demons had us surrounded. They only had to push us a little further, and we'd all go tumbling over the edge, just as Arran had.

We may have saved the other dimensions, but no one here stood a chance.

Or at least it seemed that way.

Until ...

Two amber eyes appeared in the sky, burning brightly. Pink lines traced across the darkness, eventually coalescing to reveal the outline of tapered feline face. It was dark against the gloom, yet the pink light revealed her features clearly. Bastet – the overseer of this realm and of all our souls – had recovered.

The cat goddess' voice thundered through the sky.

"This is my realm," she said. "And none of you belong here. You must return from whence you came."

Silence fell all around us. Heads turned every which way, and for a moment it seemed that everyone had forgotten that we were at the height of a battle.

Columns of light suddenly fell out of the sky. They looked like beams of sunshine pushing through a breaking cloud. Except these didn't expand from a source, but cascaded straight downwards.

They cast down upon every single entity on the battlefield. Once they found their targets, they spread out, filling us all with bright amber light.

One of these beams latched right onto my forehead. It warmed where it touched, soothed me, and healed all my aching muscles, all my pain.

I turned up to Bastet's face in the sky. It was like she was watching me. But I'm sure everyone felt the same thing. She was a goddess after all, and could control minds.

"Now go home," Bastet said.

And the darkness faded to white.

53

THE CHOICE

The brightness filled my vision to such an extent that I saw stars. I sensed my consciousness leaving my body, floating away, drifting.

"You have done the world proud, Dragoncat," said the voice of my crystal in my head.

Then came a sensation that was like being on Salanraja, when she'd suddenly accelerated into a dive. I was travelling somewhere at speed – through a portal. Perhaps through the Sixth Dimension that linked all others together.

Then it was as if I had suddenly hit a snag, because I jerked to halt.

Everything was spinning around me. I closed my eyes, then opened them again.

I was still in the Fifth Dimension. I'd travelled away from the Final Falls. A rolling landscape surrounded me, the sky having returned to its normal lilac. There was no longer any sign of a portal to the Seventh Dimension. Pink outlines traced the distant hills. Yet I stood in a valley, and two other portals stood before me.

One glowed green around its rim and led into a verdant land. It smelled of rich grass and pollen. Far away, I saw unicorns feeding on the grass, and some dragons passed overhead without disturbing the terrain.

But the other led to a familiar place with an even richer smell. There was a bowl of milk, and a second bowl of smoked salmon. Behind that was the tiled wall with the yellow stain on it I recognised. I used to eat there in that exact same spot, three times a day. The portal led to my old home, and my hackles shot up when I saw another tomcat – a regular tabby – stalk forward and feed from my bowl.

A voice came from behind me, rumbling and deep. "It seems you're still conflicted about your home, Dragoncat. That's why I couldn't send you back there."

I turned to see Bastet towering above me. She sat ramrod straight, her golden circlet gleaming.

"What is this?" I asked.

Bastet lowered her head and came down as close to level with me as she could. "I'm giving you a choice. After all you've been through, it wouldn't seem proper not to."

Whiskers, this was an incredibly cruel decision. That smoked salmon smelled delicious, and the tabby was wolfing it all down. I heard the voice of the mistress who had looked after me in South Wales laughing, and I suddenly felt horribly alone.

"I don't want to make a choice," I said. "This isn't fair."

"Oh, but you must," Bastet said. "This is the final stage of your journey. Or would you rather stay here to serve me, with the other cats? Because the portals will soon close."

"I ..." I really didn't know what to do. My whiskers twitched and my head jerked from one portal to the other.

My bond with Salanraja, my dear friends – Rine, Ange, Seramina, Asinda – and of course Aleam, who had cared for me for so long. Not to mention Esme, Pali, and good old Max.

But then I could go back to South Wales. My life there had always been easy. I'd never have to be hungry, I'd never have to worry about saving the world, and I wouldn't have to deal with smelly magical horses, ever, ever again.

It was how cats were meant to live, wasn't it?

"I would hurry up, if I were you," Bastet said. "For time is wearing thin."

The glowing rims around the portals were growing dimmer. They were wavering, and I knew this was a sign they were about to close.

"Last chance," Bastet said.

"I'm going," I snapped.

I stepped forward, then I turned back over my shoulder to add, "Thank you, Bastet."

Bastet lowered her head and blinked twice. I stepped forward once more, set my eyes on my destination, and sprinted onwards.

I had made my choice, although I knew I really didn't have one.

I made it through just before the portal closed.

54

A DELICIOUS SURPRISE

After learning of our heroism in the Fifth Dimension, King Garmin invited us to a banquet. There was meant to be food aplenty – a feast fit for even the fussiest of cats. Naturally, it was an invitation I couldn't refuse.

You couldn't fit an entire army into Cimlean Palace's grand hall, so the king didn't even try. But he did extend the invitation to all of my friends, and many of the White Mages too, including the unicorns.

Fortunately, the smell was so rich coming from the kitchens that the hall didn't smell of magical horse. It smelled herby – of the good herbs, not the bad ones – and of many different meats. Pork, chicken, duck, venison, and some kind of smoked fish – probably trout.

My mouth was watering, and it was torture waiting for the food to arrive. The king had created a high wooden chair with a table at the front of it, wide enough to accommodate three cats and a dog. Esme sat on my right, and the cheetah Palimali on my left, with Max right next to her. Pali's tummy was rumbling so loudly that I worried she might decide to eat one of us before dinner arrived.

We sat around a square wooden table, chatter rising from every direction. There were jokes, there was laughter, and there was also a string quartet playing from an alcove high above us.

Ange and Rine looked so happy sitting next to me, playfully laughing and teasing each other like old friends become lovers. Asinda sat next to Lars, and their conversation seemed less playful, but they were also happy and gazing at each other lovingly. Seramina sat next to Aleam, and she was smiling in a way that she hadn't for a long time.

The news that we'd received earlier had put us all in excellent spirits.

We'd been told that as Asinda, Seramina and I had become White Mages, and Capitut's Key had been destroyed, we no longer needed to study at the School of the White. Asinda had graduated and was to be posted to the Dragon Guard with Lars. Meanwhile Seramina, Max, and I were to return to study at Dragonsbond Academy, where we belonged.

King Garmin sat at the head of the table, bedecked in red silk brocade and hefty jewellery. His crown had so many shining and colourful gems in it that I wondered if he wore it to draw attention away from his grey hair. It was the first time I'd seen him in the flesh. He had very white teeth, and looked much healthier than Arran ever had. His cheeks shone as he talked and he was always smiling. He looked like the kind of man you'd want to know. The kind of man who would always feed you when you miaowed, and then would allow you to sleep on his lap.

You'd never think he was related to Arran just by looking at him. Alliander's kinship to the Warlock Prince I could believe, but not this kind-hearted king's.

Alliander sat on one side of the king, together with some important-looking White Mage officials. She didn't smile at all, just kept nodding her head and making the occasional comment when someone spoke to her. She didn't look at any of us, the dark mages who had once run away from the School of the White.

Some of the leaders of the Dragon Guard sat on the other side of the king. The Council of Three were also there. The great bald giant, Driar Brigel, and the stout Driar Lonamm looked like they were enjoying themselves. But the gaunt Driar Yila had her usual harsh stare as she looked around her. I guess she wasn't one for social occasions.

Alas, our dragons weren't here but in the next room, where the king's dragon, Charmins, was entertaining them. Salanraja had already told me that this was a time to be alone with her kind and had asked me kindly to stay out of her mind.

They were up to something – I was sure of it. I just had no idea what it was.

Esme leaned over and touched her nose to my cheek. I turned to her and she blinked her bright blue eyes slowly at me.

"We did well," she said. "We deserve this."

"But the food still isn't here yet," I said. "When will they finally do their job and finish cooking?"

"One day, Ben, you'll learn how to be patient."

"Cats aren't meant to be patient. We're meant to want food as soon as we see it. I mean look at Palimali over there – she's famished."

Palimali turned her head.

"Are you two talking about me?"

She didn't speak the cat language, so she wouldn't understand a word we said.

"Just saying how hungry you must be," I replied in the cheetah tongue. "Isn't that right, Pali?"

"Of course I am ... I just wish you hadn't put me next to this slobbering dog."

"What's that?" Max whined softly. "Speak in the dog language so I can understand."

"Nothing," I barked back, and the room fell silent for a moment.

I guess many of the patrons hadn't expected to share company with a barking cat.

"Say," I said, turning back to Esme. "We never found out what Lasinta was up to."

Esme twitched her whiskers. "Up to no good, I suspect."

"But should we be worried about it? She touched the King's Crystal for a reason. I mean, does anyone other than Seramina, Asinda, you and me actually know she was there?"

"Not yet," Esme said. "But let's deal with that issue after our feast."

"But what if she does something while we're eating? What if she's planning to do something to us in this room right now?"

"Will you just shut up, Ben?" Esme asked.

I frowned at her.

"It's just that you're always so worried and anxious. Try to enjoy the celebration."

"I will when the food arrives," I said. "By the way, I wonder what happened to Rex and his colony. The King of Cats."

"I've heard a rumour," Esme said, "that they'll be sent the leftovers."

That made me happy. They certainly deserved it. After all, they had done their job and done it well.

I turned my attention towards the room.

I couldn't help but think about Ta'ra, then – my Cat Sidhe companion. That fairy prince, Ta'lon, had stolen her away from me.

I just hoped that she was happy, because it couldn't be easy pretending that you're a fairy when you're really a cat.

Still, I had Esme as a companion now, and I could tell she cared. She had taught me how to be a White Mage. I guessed I could be happy with her – at least for the time being.

After we had waited a short while, King Garmin stood up. He raised a golden goblet and tapped it loudly with his fork. I flattened my ears against my head – I'd had enough of loud noises during the battle.

"May I have your attention, please," King Garmin said.

One of the white mages, a woman, shouted out from the other side of the table, "Speech!"

King Garmin laughed, displaying all his teeth.

"We'll have time for speeches later. For now, I want you to enjoy a special feast we've prepared as an *aperitif*. I believe you've tried many things, but this is something sourced especially from our envoys in the Fourth Dimension, that most of you have never tried. One of our heroes here is particularly partial to it, I believe. Roasted by the fiery breath of all of our dragons present, this is going to be a fine feast indeed."

King Garmin looked at me and winked. I blinked back, slowly, wondering if my dream were finally coming true.

The king turned back to the archway, from where the smell of delicious food was wafting out. A serving maid came through the entrance, pulling behind her a trolley with a massive, covered silver dish on top. She navigated it over to a gap in the tables and placed it in the centre of the room.

"The problem with this dish," the king said, "is that if you paired it with a girl named Ella, you'll end up with food poisoning."

The room gave a laugh, but it was only from politeness. I'm not sure anyone got the joke, including me. I didn't care anyway. All my focus was on the silver platter, and the smoky smell that drifted out from underneath the lid.

It was really happening. My dream was finally coming true.

The serving maid lifted the lid, revealing a long and meaty fish stretched along the silver plate. It had very sharp teeth. Four silver bowls lay before it.

"Let's give the treat to our brave animals first," King Garmin said, and he turned to me, again displaying a toothy grin.

I miaowed at the serving maid. I don't know if it was to say thank you or hurry up; I can't remember.

The serving maid lifted the bowls, two in each hand. I was salivating as she brought them forwards. Her journey from the serving tray to our makeshift table took far too long for my comfort.

But eventually she put them down on the table before us. Four bowls, each with hot smoked salmon, served only with a little pepper and dill.

I didn't care what was going on in the room after that, for my head was already in my bowl, and I was the happiest cat in all of the eight dimensions, and I'm sure I proved that by the volume of my purr.

ACKNOWLEDGMENTS

THE ACKNOWLEDGEMENTS SECTION of a book is one of my favourites to write. I find it immensely gratifying to think through everyone who has helped out. I couldn't have come so far in this journey as an author by myself; many have helped me along the way.

Firstly, special thanks to Tarryn Thomas for her excellent copy-editing and proofreading work. Honestly, I can't thank you enough for the professional polish you've added to the work, and I admire how you've managed to do get there through so many power outages.

I also wanted to thank Carol Brandon and Wayne M. Scace for all the help you've given during this series and my other works. Your input has been incredibly valuable, and I couldn't express that enough.

As always, thank you also to my family, especially my parents who are always there supporting me. Of course, I'd be remiss if I didn't mention my dear wife Ola for reading the early drafts, pointing out when Ben goes a little over the top with things, and just generally being a wonderful support. You deserve more than a thousand thank yous, delivered in chocolate parcels.

Thank you also to everyone on my ARC team. The help that you've given me throughout my career has been invaluable.

Finally, thank you to every single reader for all the work to support indie authors like myself and the world of literature at large.

THANK YOU FOR READING "*A Cat's Guide to Vanquishing Evil*". I hope that you enjoyed it and that it added value for you in your every day life.

I have written a prequel novelette to this novel entitled "*A Cat's Guide to Serving a Warlock*", which you can download for free by signing up to my newsletter at https://chrisbehrsin.com/servingawarlock.

I send bi-monthly emails with promos, giveaways, information about new releases and news about what's going on in my life in general.